Bloody Commas 3

Lock Down Publications and Ca$h
Presents
Bloody Commas 3
A Novel by *T.J. Edwards*

Lock Down Publications
Po Box 870494
Mesquite, Tx 75187

Visit our site at www.lockdownpublications.com

Copyright 2018 by Bloody Commas 3 T.J. Edwards

Lock Down Publications
Like our page on Facebook: Lock Down Publications @
www.facebook.com/lockdownpublications.ldp
Cover design and layout by: **Dynasty Cover Me**
Book interior design by: **Shawn Walker**
Edited by**: Tisha Andrews**

Stay Connected with Us!

Text **LOCKDOWN** to 22828 to stay up-to-date
with new releases, sneak peaks, contests and more…
Thank you!

Submission Guideline

Submit the first three chapters of your completed manuscript to ldpsubmissions@gmail.com, subject line: Your book's title. The manuscript must be in a .doc file and sent as an attachment. Document should be in Times New Roman, double spaced and in size 12 font. Also, provide your synopsis and full contact information. If sending multiple submissions, they must each be in a separate email.

Have a story but no way to send it electronically? You can still submit to LDP/Ca$h Presents. Send in the first three chapters, written or typed, of your completed manuscript to:

LDP: Submissions Dept
Po Box 870494
Mesquite, Tx 75187

DO NOT send original manuscript. Must be a duplicate.

Provide your synopsis and a cover letter containing your full contact information.

Thanks for considering LDP and Ca$h Presents.

Dedications

This book is dedicated to my wife, who is so stomp down on all levels. You're the only true Queen that's fit to sit beside a man like me. I'd splash a hunnit niggaz for you with no hesitation because your loyalty is real, and that's why I keep you spoiled. I love you, Mrs. Jelissa Edwards.

It's also dedicated to our mother in heaven. Mrs. Deborah Lin Edwards. Rest in Peace, Momma. Soon as I touch down in 2019, I'm buying you that grave plot that you deserve.

Rae'Jon and A'Jhani, Daddy crazy about the both of you. I know it's wild having a goon for a father, but we'll figure it out. I got the both of you for life. Soon as y'all old enough to drive, I'm putting you in somethin' foreign. Your bank accounts will stay straight. The future is yours.

Acknowledgments

I pledge allegiance to the homie, Cash. I'd make them hammers bark for you. Ain't no mafucka was trying to give me and my wife a chance before you stepped in and put that cake up taking a chance on us. For that alone, I'm with you until the end, and I'll face that Reaper with you. My loyalty sealed in blood. All the commas we seeing now is because you took that chance. I ain't never met a nigga that was one hunnit, until you introduced yourself. I'ma keep this pen bleeding for you and treat it as my hammer so I can make sure that I'm doing my part for the family.

Shawn, you are a true goddess, and it goes further than what you do for the company. You got a crazy ass brother that's coming home in 2019, so them kats out there better beware. You are the truth, my sister, and I appreciate how you hold me and my wife down. Our loyalty for you is sealed in blood, and ain't nothing we won't do for you. Love you, Goddess.

Lastly, to everybody that doubted me, thank you. A hustler needs motivation, and mine came from my own blood-line. Now watch them numbers add up.

Jehovah is real!

T.J. EDWARDS

Chapter 1

"That's how it has to go. There is absolutely no way around it. I want you to murder him, then take care of his entire crew and I need this done before the month is out," Kabir said, looking directly into King's eyes.

There wasn't any other American that he trusted more than him. King had a reputation that preceded him all the way to the Middle East.

King clenched his jaw. There was no doubt in his mind that he was up for the task. Kabir had pulled enough strings to get him released. Now he was asking him to pay his debt. He wanted Greed and his entire crew murdered.

Kabir leaned into his ear. "The bounty is five million dollars if you can complete the task in less than thirty days. If you can do it before then, you'll get ten. You have two point five million that has already been made available to you. The end of his life is very important to me and a few more higher ups. You take care of this the right way and The Underworld will be placed at your feet. He is an animal, so you'll have to be relentless. You were looking for a way into ISIS. Well, here is your key."

King clenched his jaw and slowly nodded his head. He had heard a lot about the infamous Greed. They were no strangers to each other. Greed operated out of the east coast and King was strongly in the Midwest, deeply rooted in the city of Chicago where he was a living street legend.

He decided he would use this green light to not only take out Greed and his entire organization, but also to gain a strong hold on the east coast. Then for him, all that would be left was the south and Big Meech. He curled his lip at the thought of him. Yeah, he would fulfill the contract on Greed immediately.

***

Three more days passed by before they were able to have Stacey's funeral. It was a windy and very snowy day. The mood for the entire family was down, all having heavy hearts for the woman coupled with the loss of Jahni. The service lasted two hours. Averie's family had flown from all around the country just to be present. When it was all said and done, many hugs had been given and numerous tears shed.

Ajani had had enough of all the mushy shit. He felt like he needed a break from it all, so he tapped Vanity on the thigh. She gave him a crazy look. "I need for you to move a lil' bit so I can get out of this church. I need some air."

Vanity squeezed his hand in understanding. She stood up, allowing him to get out of the   section where they were sitting inside the church. She hugged him and kissed his cheek. "Don't worry about it, baby. Tonight, me and Dior gon' do whatever it takes to make you feel all better. Whatever you want, you gon' get. I promise. You hear me?" She kissed his cheek again, her perfume wafting up his nose.

Even though they were at a funeral, Ajani still found himself getting excited, imagining what he was going to have them do.

He hugged her before making his way outside of the church. He took a fat blunt from the   inside of his coat pocket and opened the doors to the church.

As soon as he did, his eyes got as big as paper plates. The last thing he remembered was wishing he'd put on his bulletproof vest that morning before the rapid shots spit down on him.

***

Rayjon heard all the gunfire. He pushed Averie to the floor before pulling his twin .45s out of their holsters. He could hear people dropping to the floor along with screams of panic. They were under attack by what sounded like an entire fucking army.

***

Greed made Jersey get down and slammed the magazines into his Glock .40s. His heart was beating loudly in his chest. As his eyes scanned the entire church, the windows shattered and bullets came flying inside, chopping up the wooden pews. There was a loud boom. Then the church was on fire with people running around engulfed in flames. He had to figure out the   attack as they were coming at him hard.

***

King sent ten more men to the back of the church after giving them the order to go in and kill everybody in sight. He took the grenade out of the bag and squeezed it in his hand. There would be no way he was going to allow Greed to escape his impending demise.

"Nigga, I'm sendin' you to your muthafuckin' maker!" he gritted.

He was sure this would end in a total victory. Not once did he consider that he might fail, and Greed would escape his wrath. But even the best laid out plans don't always bear ripened fruit. King curled his lip and proceeded with his mission only to encounter the totally unexpected.

Chapter 2

Boooom!

"Arrrrgh! Help me! I'm on fire!" Deacon Blakemore yelled, running through the aisles with his entire back ablaze.

He was a deacon at the First Baptist Church of New Jersey, currently the building that held Stacey's deceased body and the building that was in that moment, under attack.

"Help me! Please, somebody!" he hollered, completely ablaze now. It looked painful to watch. You could hear his skin frying depending on how close you were. Deacon Blakemore felt the fire scorching his skin away. The pain was unbearable. It felt like he was being peeled alive by a bunch of small potato peelers. He could hear himself sizzling like bacon. The fire shot all up his neck hurting so bad, he started begging for Jesus to take him home.

"Take me, Lord! Take me now! Please!" he wailed at the top of his lungs.

Boom! Boom! Boom!

The windows shattered at the top of the church and then another cocktail was thrown through one of them. It hit the hardwood floor and exploded, sending flames to shoot into the air.

Greed threw his body on top of Jersey as a glass window shattered, and the shards landed on his back. He didn't care what was about to take place. He knew that he would give his life to protect his wife. She was his everything.

Boom! Boom! Boom! Shhhh! Booom!

One of the benches exploded and flew into the

air. It landed on top of Stacey's casket, knocking it over. She rolled half way out of it and a woman screamed.

Rayjon kept his body firmly on top of Averie. He knew they had to get out of there or it would be all over for them. He didn't know what was going on, but his common sense told him they were under attack. The only person that crossed his mind that would be coming for them like that was Envy, but his parents reassured him he was already dead. So he wondered what was going on or if maybe they had missed something.

Jersey tried to get Greed up off her. The heat was getting intense. Every time she inhaled, it felt like she was breathing in fire. They had to get out of that church and fast. She didn't know who they were up against, but she knew her husband would have it all under control once they were able to regroup.

"Greed, let me up! We gotta get out of here!"

Boom! Boom! Boom!

"Arrrrgh!"

"Noooo!" A fat older man screamed and ran to his wife's side as she fell flat on her face. Her big church hat flew off, ending up in the aisle on fire.

"Jersey, chill. These mafuckas can't keep bussing forever. We gotta let them run out of ammo," Greed said, although he knew that wasn't the smartest move.

He knew at any moment, they could've kicked in the door and bum rushed them, killing any and everybody in sight. They were caught off guard and the way it sounded, they were   completely out numbered. For the first time in his life, he feared not being able to protect his family. He almost felt emasculated.

Jersey tried to wiggle from underneath him. "No, get off me! I gotta find Rayjon and Ajani! Then we can hit it out of the cellar that's in the back of the church. Get off me!"

She pushed him off with all her might and shot up, looking for her children. "Rayjon! Ajani! Where are you, babies? Can you hear my voice?"

She was looking all around. It had to be at least fifteen people lying on the floor dead or on their way there. Somewhere in the fire while others were bled out from gunshot wounds, tears fell down her face as she scanned over the entire church looking for her sons.

Sssshhhhh! Boooom!

The entire pulpit blew up along with where the choir usually sang their songs, turning into fire. Jersey was knocked off her feet and was thrown backwards. When she landed, she hit her head hard against one of the wooden benches and blacked out.

Greed scooped her up into his arms, taking off as he ran behind Averie and Rayjon who were holding hands as they headed for the back of the church. The entire inside was filled with thick clouds of smoke and fire. It was nearly impossible to breathe. His lungs felt like he was inhaling acid. The only thing on his mind was getting his wife to safety.

Rayjon pulled Averie by the hand, leading her down the stairs and into the hallway where the bathrooms were located. Growing up in New Jersey, his parents made it a rule that he and Ajani had to sing in the choir and attend church every single Sunday.

So he knew that building by hard.

There was only one other way to exit the church if you did not leave from the upstairs of the building. That way was located in the basement. Down there was the part of the church where the youth choir usually practiced in the afternoons after school. You could also meet there with a few adults that would help you with your homework.

"Come on, Pops! Just keep on following me!" he yelled over his shoulder.

Greed had no other choice. He had been to the church a few times, but he had never been downstairs, so he didn't know where his son was taking him. Yet he trusted him one hundred percent. Averie was scared out of her mind. She didn't know what to think or what to do. She felt like she was about to pass out. The smoke was everywhere, making it nearly impossible to breathe. She prayed that Ajani was okay. She prayed that nothing happened to him. Then she thought about her son, Jahni and immediately became sick to her stomach. They hadn't even had the opportunity to bury him correctly and now this.

She didn't know what the family had gotten themselves into, but lately she started to feel the need to get away from them and fast. But her only anchor was Rayjon. She had fallen so deeply for him, she felt like she would've done anything for or with him. She would even follow him all the way to the grave if she had to.

They made it all the way to the back of the basement. Rayjon saw the exit that led out of the cellar was blocked by a bunch of picnic tables.

"Come on, Pops. We gotta move these tables. Get up out here before this whole building blows." He ran over and started pulling the tables away from the exit.

Greed laid Jersey down on the floor a safe distance away from the tables. Then he ran over and started to help his son. The more tables they moved, the madder he got. He had to find out who it was that was attacking them.

* * *

"Blow that muthafucka up, Joe! Burn that bitch to the ground! I want this bitch ass nigga dead!"

King took the pin out of the grenade, dropping it to the ground before taking the explosive and throwing it through the window inside of the church. He jogged back to the street and stood behind his truck. He could hear a bunch of sirens in the background, knowing then he had to get his crew out of there. He barely knew anything about New Jersey.

He was from Chicago, Illinois, the land of Lincoln. His sole purpose for being anywhere on the east coast was to annihilate Greed and wipe out his entire family. Those were the orders given to him by Kabir the Arab and those were the orders he intended to follow with everything that he had.

He ducked down and braced himself.

Whoooom!

The church exploded into a big ball of fire. Huge pieces of wood and siding flew into the air before crashing down to the earth. King figured there was no way anyone could have survived that blast. But just to be sure, his Young Radicals pumped another 300 rounds into what was left of the building before jumping into their S.U.V.s and smashing away. King planned on wiping out their entire bloodline. He didn't care where he started, but before he left New Jersey, he was going to make it his business to kill as many of them as possible.

* * *

Ajani continued to run down the alley as fast as he could. He had been shot four times in the midsection and twice in the back. Even though he wore a bulletproof vest, it still felt like a few bullets had made it all the way through.

He could taste the blood in his mouth, his vision becoming blurry. He tried to force his body to fight and move forward. He had to get away from the church. The church was where the enemy was. He needed to live, so he had to keep on running as far as he could until he no longer could.

* * *

"Arghhh!" Rayjon screamed. The explosion had knocked them off their feet as if a bus had hit them. Rayjon landed first, hard on his side. He heard his rib pop, pain shooting all throughout his body. "Arrgh! Shit!" he hollered just as Averie fell beside him.

She landed with a thud, her head bouncing off the concrete before she rolled on to her side knocked out cold. Rayjon crawled to her immediately. He leaned down and put his ear to her chest, trying to see if her heart was still beating. After confirming it was, he picked her up and cradled her into his arms.

Jersey landed on top of a plastic green garbage can with Greed falling a split second after her. He landed on the concrete of the alley. He tried to break his fall with his hand but ended up twisting it awkwardly, skinning up his entire right arm. He rolled on to his side in so much pain, he wanted to holler but instead he jumped up and ran over to Jersey. He knelt beside her to make sure she was okay.

She laid on her back, groaning in pain. "Ajani? Ajani? Rayjon? Where are you, babies? I don't want you to die," she whimpered with her eyes closed.

Greed kissed her on the forehead and rubbed her cheek. "Get up, baby. We gotta go.   Everybody gone be okay. We just gotta get out of here."

He texted Aiden again, letting him know where they were. He did it twice before in the church but hadn't gotten a response. It was unlike his nephew. He needed him more than ever. They could hear what sounded like a million sirens getting closer.

The snow started to fall heavily, and the wind picked up. As soon as everyone got to their feet, they started to make their way down the alley. They had to get as far away from the sirens as possible. The last thing they needed was to be apprehended by the authorities. Even though all of them were seriously injured, seeking that kind of help was not an option. The family had committed too many crimes to risk it.

* * *

Aiden jumped out of the truck, helping them put Ajani in the back of it. He noted his cousin was bloody, going in and out of consciousness. His heart felt heavy. He wanted to know what happened to him. He felt like he had failed all of them. He put him in the backseat and strapped the seatbelt around him before checking the text on his phone to read Greed's iPhone 8 location.

Chapter 3

King took the razor blade and chopped through the pile of cocaine. He had four ounces poured out on the mirror, making four thick lines before he tooted one hard, sniffing it straight to the head. He coughed, pinched his nose together, and leaned down, treating the other nostril with a fluffy line of powder.

"Mafuckas think I came all way out here to play games, Chris. This nigga Greed think it's sweet." He leaned down to toot up another line.

Chris was King's right-hand man. They had been best friends ever since they were four years old. Their mother used to bathe them in the same bathtub. After King was indicted, it was Chris that held down the fort. He kept the supply of the Virgin running heavily throughout the city of Chicago. Both men were relentless and extremely cold-hearted. All they cared about were large sums of money and their children.

King, however, had one additional weakness by the name of China. She too had grown up alongside of them ever since she was four years old. But somewhere along the way, she'd become King's baby mother and his first true love. Chris tooted a thick line of the cocaine and threw back a shot of Hennessy.

"You already know I don't like these east coast niggas anyway. These fuck niggas think we ain't 'bout that life down there in the Land." He stopped to toot another line of cocaine before leaning back on the couch and sipping from the bottle of Hennessy.

"So, you already know I'm ready to make our

presence felt around here, especially if it means you don't owe that towel head shit else." King nodded.

"When it's all said and done, we gone have to kill his ass, too. You know ain't no such thing as us leaving any loose ends. That's the first rule of the game." King tooted a line hard. The cocaine felt like it shot into his brain and got stuck as soon as it got to its destination, sending strong jolts of euphoria all throughout him. He couldn't help but to smile. His heart was beating faster than a drummer on steroids.

Chris flipped on the big screen television that was in the suite of the Bellagio hotel they were staying at. After watching it for a few minutes, he frowned.

"Bro, I don't think we got that nigga," he said, sounding worried.

King coughed and punched himself in the chest. The cocaine had him feeling like a champion.

"What you talkin' about?" he asked, turning towards the television screen, reading the bottom of it.

They were announcing some of the people that had been hurt in the attack, even flashing their pictures across the screen. None of them had been Greed nor anybody in his family as far as King knew, but he wasn't sure. They reported there were still two other bodies that were remained unidentified but would keep the public up to speed with the case when more details became available. They deemed the attack a religious hate crime. That was the only part of the report that made King smile.

Chris stood up and lit a cigarette and said, "If we missed that nigga, then that mean we gone have to stick around for a minute. What that even look like?"

King continued to watch the news after hitting

the mute button. "My orders were to wipe out this nigga whole family, so that's definitely what I'm about to do. I say we tear this muthafucka up, then go back home like bosses. I miss Chicago already." He leaned down and tooted another healthy line of dope.

Chris didn't like the feel of warring with an enemy on their turf. He felt like they were out of bounds. Besides, the war thing wasn't his cup of tea. He wasn't ducking no action but at the same time, he was all about getting rich, watching his money pile as high as the ceiling. But on the other hand, King was his nigga and he needed him sitting on top of the throne of their dynasty. His knowledge of the game was incredible and had them eating like gods ever since they were young teenagers.

"Bra, to be honest with you, I'm down to do whatever you want to do just as long as you're sure you got shit under control.

King laughed, pinching his nose before running his tongue across his teeth. "I gotta hold up my end on everything, so we gone fuck this nigga over and murder his bloodline. Then after we fulfill this contract, we going back to the Windy City and continue getting rich, but first things first." He stood up and turned off the television, throwing the remote on the bed. "Let's find out where this nigga people stay. If he think he gone hide out until we leave, he got another thing coming. The best way to make a mark come out of hiding is to start whacking the family. So that's what we gone do. All it's gone take is one week for us to finish this nigga off, then we back to the Land."

Chris cocked back the Mack and shrugged his shoulders. "You already know I'm riding wit' you until the wheels fall off. Let's make this muthafucka the murder capitol of the world.   Chicago Style."

* * *

"Ahhhh! Shit! What the fuck are you doing to me?" Ajani hollered as tears ran down his cheeks. He had never been in more pain than he was right in that moment.

"Boy, if you curse in front of me one more time, I swear I'm gone shoot yo' ass up myself. Now, be still! It's almost out! Take this like a man and thank Jehovah that you're even alive," Jersey said, digging into his back with the surgery pick to pry the bullet out of his muscle. She almost had it before he jerked, making her grip slip off.

"My bad, momma, but this is killing me. Somebody gotta at least give me a Percocet, some methadone or something," he said, wincing in pain. He felt her digging into his back again with the pick. He clenched his teeth together to keep from hollering at the top of his lungs.

Greed paced back and forth in front of Aiden with his arm heavily wrapped. The fall had taken a nice amount of his skin off. His family was under attack and he knew it was his job to figure out what was going on. He tried to think of every enemy he had in the area. Their ranking amongst the Underworld. Their firepower. Their level of hate for him. Their race, everything. Mentally he was not leaving any stone unturned. There had to be a logical explanation for what was going on and he needed to find it.

Aiden sat quietly, wondering what was going on inside of his uncle's head. Whenever he saw him pacing back and forth, he knew he was lost in deep thought. That meant he knew their backs were against the wall as he tried to find a solution that would fit, allowing their family to prevail victoriously. He was more than ready to put in some work. He didn't know who had attacked them, but they had hurt his family. In his mind, that meant that a whole lot of people had to pay.

Greed stopped in mid stride. "That nigga, Money."

Aiden lowered his eyes and frowned. "Huh?"

"That nigga Money outta Jamaica, Queens. That nigga just came into a bunch of cash from all that music shit, right?"

Aiden nodded, "Yeah, I heard they dropped a million in his lap."

Greed clapped his hands together. "That nigga always said that when he got his chips up, he was gone come at me hard. I couldn't kill his bitch ass back then because we were both in the hole in Sing-Sing, but I never forgot about that shit. One thing you always gotta remember, don't forget the threats people make towards you. It's imperative that you remember every single one. And if you can, as soon as a mafucka threaten you, you take they ass out the game right then and there. Remember, the golden rule is that you never threaten any man and never allow a mafucka to know your next move or what you're thinking, especially an enemy."

Aiden jumped up off the couch and stood up. "So, you want me to go finish this nigga?" He put on his black gloves and wiggled his fingers. "I know it's my fault that he's still alive, but Unk, you gotta know that I popped this nigga nine times. The way he was twisted on that   concrete, it looked like Sun was outta there."

Greed frowned. "That's why you always check for a pulse. I told you that time and time again. If you don't check for a pulse, you fuck 'em over in a way to make sure they ain't never getting back up." He slapped his hands together again in anger. "That bitch ass nigga. That's the only person it could be, too. Well, if that's how he wanna play shit, fucking with my family while we already grieving over one loved one, then that's on him. But that just means that his family ain't safe either. Let's turn the fuck up, nephew."

Aiden nodded his head. "What's first?"

Jersey took the bullet out of Ajani's back and dropped it into the metal bowl on the side of her before stitching him up. "I ain't never seen nobody cry as much as you do, Sun. I'm so   disappointed right now."

Jersey shook her head in irritation. She expected more from her younger son. She felt he should have been thankful to be alive instead of whimpering while she took bullets out of him. Getting shot was a part of the game and her family was supposed to be prepared for this fate,   especially after all the people they had shot or killed.

It was impossible to go through life the way that they did without being on the receiving end. Karma was a bitch and deep down in Jersey's heart, she felt like things were about to get ten times worse for them. She had visions of death. She felt it in her stomach that there was about to be a lot of bloodshed. When it was all said and done, she knew a few of those in her family would no longer be breathing. It saddened her, but at the same time, she was mentally preparing herself for it.

Ajani jumped off the table, wrapping his arms around her before kissing her on both cheeks. "I love you, momma. I ain't mean to sound all weak and stuff but trying to endure this with no pain medication is crazy." He felt extremely dizzy. The places she had dug the bullets out of were screaming in pain. He wanted to faint, but he tried his best to keep it together in front of her.

Jersey pointed to Greed and Aiden. "Go over there and see where you're needed. Somebody is attacking this family and I know your father is over there trying to figure it out. Go help."

She grabbed all the medical supplies, preparing to take them back upstairs to her mother's house. They were in her big basement while she was up in the kitchen cooking a full course meal. If there was one thing that Sadie knew how to do, it was get down in that kitchen and even though Jersey felt sick to her stomach, she felt there was always room for her mother's good home cooking.

Chapter 4

"Come here, baby. I don't like when you get to sitting in the dark and shit. I need you to talk   to me," Rayjon said, kneeling down and taking Averie by the hand, pulling her up.

She wrapped her arms around his neck and started to cry. "I'm so scared, baby. I don't know what to do. Something is telling me to get out of here, but I don't want to lose you. You're all I have right now, and I need you just to have a reason to stay alive because I'm so lost." She   started sobbing in his ear.

Rayjon held her more tightly before kissing her on the neck, then sucking and biting into it. "You thinking about leaving me? Huh?" He sucked and licked her harder, then picked her up so she could wrap her legs around him. "You already know how this family get down and now you ready to leave us?" He sucked on her neck so hard, she moaned in pain.

Averie then threw her head back. "No, baby. I'm not saying that I wanna leave you. I'm just—Uh!"

Rayjon threw her on the bed and closed the door behind him. After taking off his shirt and vest, he threw them on the floor. His ribs were heavily taped and even though he felt severe pain, he paid it no mind. "It's only one way I'm gone get yo' ass to thinking something else because it ain't even going down like that."

Averie looked up at him with lust and fear in her eyes. She didn't know what he was going to do, but she was excited. She wanted him to take the wheel, to give her a reason to stay beside him. She needed to know that he needed her.

Rayjon straddled her, ripping off her blouse. He then took her bra, doing the same before throwing it over his shoulder. Her titties jiggled on her chest. They were nice, brown, and round, with thick nipples that stood at attention. He cupped them and pushed them together. "You think you about to take these perfect titties away from me. Don't you know I love these mafuckas?"

He leaned down and sucked the left nipple into his mouth, pulling on it with his teeth, sending chills all throughout her body. Averie arched her back and moaned into the air. To her,   nobody could do her body like Rayjon could. Nobody.

"Ummm, baby. I just need you. Please," she moaned barely above a whisper.

Rayjon sucked the right nipple into his mouth and followed the same routine with his teeth. He loved the taste of her skin. He loved how her breast felt in his hands, heavy and warm. And even though they had already confessed how they felt about each other to his brother and had been given the nod, in his mind, Averie was still forbidden pussy. Just the fact that he was able to do what he was about to do was enough to drive him crazy. He pulled her skirt up to her waist and reached in between them, pulling her panties to the side before feeling all over her wet lips.

"Ummm, Shit, daddy." Averie opened her legs wider as she felt Rayjon playing and rubbing on her pussy. She could feel her juices coming out of her, wetting up her ass. She was so wet that she was aching inside.

Rayjon lifted her knees and pushed them to her chest, bussing her pussy wide open. As soon as he had her into position, he dived into her kitty as if he were starving. Spreading her lips apart, he loudly slurped up her essence before trapping her clitoris with his thick lips. He sucked with just enough force, rocking her into her first orgasm."

"Uhhh, uhhh, uhhh, Rayyyjonnnnn!" she screamed and opened her legs wider while he continued to suck her clit, fingering her at full speed. The noises he made between her thighs were driving her crazy.

As soon as she finished shaking, he stood up and stroked his big dick. Taking the juices from her pussy, he rubbed them into his stalk for lubrication.

"I want some of that pussy, Averie. I want some of that pussy right now because we could have been dead, but we ain't." He knelt on the bed, spreading her legs wide before putting her knees on her shoulders. He could smell her pussy in the air and it was intoxicating. He felt there was no other scent in the world like the natural smell of pussy.

Averie put her hand between her legs, spreading her sex lips apart as she felt his big head push into her. "Uhhh! Shit, Rayjon! Please take it easy, baby. I just need you to make love to me because I'm hurting so bad right now," she cried. "I need you."

Rayjon slid all the way home, then pulled his dick all the way back until just his head was on her sex lips. Then he slid all the way back inside again. The way her tight muscles sucked at him and her warmth engulfed his dick, made him want to stay inside of her forever. "I got you, boo. Just let daddy handle this pussy. I know what I'm doing. I need you just as much, so we can take it slow. We got all night, I promise."

* * *

Miles felt the blade slam into his shoulder as the masked man ripped it downward, slicing a part the muscle. As soon as he felt the blood pouring out of him, he threw his head back and started to holler into the duct tape. "Arrrrrgh! Arrrgh! Arrrgh!"

Before he could get used to that attack, the same knife slammed into his shoulder again, but this time it felt like the blade went way deeper as the man was trying to pull and rip his arm off. He forced it upward, then twisted it again and again. He could literally hear his bones popping. The pain was so intense, he felt he was about to pass out.

King smacked him so hard, he yelped out in pain. "Wake yo' bitch ass up and take this shit like a man!" He twisted his arm again and again, then started yanking it to his chest. It still wouldn't come off, so he took the knife and slammed it back into his shoulder, pulling   downward. As he sliced and dug. he felt the blade hit the bone. Then he slammed his hand on top of the handle and jammed it into him even harder.

Miles was in so much pain, he shitted on himself. He had never in his life felt anything like it. The blade felt like it was scraping against his bone. He could feel it hitting it. He wanted to die.

"Hold this bitch nigga, Joe," King ordered.

Chris came over and held Miles's head while King yanked at his arm as hard as he could. The arm started to slowly come a loose at the shoulder. It was now hanging on by the bone. King twisted it repeatedly until it popped loudly. Then he yanked it with all his might and it came away gushing out blood.

Miles felt him pulling and pulling and every time he pulled, the pain was so intense that it nearly made him go blind. Screaming only made it worse. When he felt the turning of his arm over and over again, he threw up in his mouth, nearly choking on it.

Nothing in his life had ever prepared him for the intense pain that he was experiencing. He heard his bones pop, then disconnect. It felt like his shoulder was being separated. The man continued to twist and pull. The pain got so bad, he shitted on himself again, then he looked down and saw his entire arm was no longer attached to his body.

Blood spurted into the air like a geyser or fire hydrant that was turned on, except his shoulder was not spewing water, but blood.

King took his arm and held it up against his shoulder like it was a sword or something. "Miles, Miles, Miles. It's fucked up you gotta go through this, but it's the price you pay for being related to Greed."

Miles's face was covered in sweat. He smelled like pure shit and ass. He was in so much pain that it made it hard to register to his brain. He heard his cousin's name, but he didn't even care. He wanted to die.

King threw Miles's arm on to the ground and grabbed him by the throat. "Where the fuck is he?"

Blood continued to shoot out of him. He was getting so dizzy that nothing was making sense. The masked man was fading in and out. It was like the world was upside down. he could feel the heat on his face from King's breath, but it didn't register that the man was in his face.

King took the knife and slammed it into Miles's thigh, causing him to scream into the tape.

He started mumbling right away, trying to tell it all. While at first nothing registered, it was now all starting to make sense. They were doing this to him because they wanted to know where Greed was. Even though he didn't know for sure, he was going to tell them everywhere he thought the man could be without leaving out a single spot.

As soon as King removed the tape from his mouth, that's exactly what he did. He told him every location that came to mind. After he was done talking, he passed out. King then left him in the abandoned building just like that after carving the name "Greed" on his forehead.

* * *

Rayjon turned her on her side and slow stroked her deeply. His dick continued to hit the   bottom while she cried and begged him to do her harder. Her pussy seemed as if it was getting hotter and hotter.

"I love it so much, baby. Aww, this dick so good. I love it so much. Kill it, daddy. I need you to kill it for me like you always do. Take me away from this pain, please." Rayjon put her thick thighs into his forearms and started ramming his dick into her at full speed.

Smack! Smack! Smack! Smack! Smack!

His head beat down her walls while his balls

slammed into her ass. The juices pouring out of her pussy made a huge puddle underneath them. The headboard rocked into the wall, making it sound like somebody was repeatedly beating on the door. He yanked her head back by her hair and bit into her neck.

"This my muthafucking pussy. You hear me? From now on, you belong to me. I need you beside me because you my baby. You got that?"

Averie screamed and bounced back into him. "Yes! Yes, daddy! Oh shit, yes! I'll do   anything you say! I need you. Heal me," she screamed again. "Rayjon! Fuck me from the back. Let me get on my knees for you, daddy. Please, I wanna get on my knees for you. I want you to really hit this shit."

Rayjon pulled out and his dick stood straight up in the air against his stomach. It glistened from her juices, smelling just like the deepest regions of her pussy. The scent drove him crazy.

Averie got up and put her face in the bed, holding her ass open for him. She pulled her cheeks apart, exposing all her essence. She felt him get behind her, running his dick up and down her crease, before slamming into her like a savage. "Ahhh! Yes! Oh shit! Yes, daddy! Fuck me like you supposed to!"

Rayjon grabbed her and pulled her into him so hard, it knocked him backwards a little bit. Then he got to killing that pussy. "Uhh! Damn, this that shit right here! Averie, you got this shit right here!" he groaned.

Averie was in a zone, bouncing back into him with her eyes closed. She was trying to release all her heartache and pain on his stick. Tears ran out of her eyes as she envisioned everything that was breaking her down from the loss of her son, to her cousin, to the position she found herself in inside of their family. All that pain was silently killing her.

Rayjon pulled her head and dog fucked her like a maniac. Her pussy was so good. The way it gripped him and the feel of her soft, hot ass bouncing back into him was the best feeling in the world to him. He felt like he could never get tired of it. He was also developing feelings for Averie that he couldn't understand. But it seemed like the more they went through something together, the crazier he became over her.

* * *

"Baby, come here. I need you to sit down and talk to me," Jersey said, pulling Greed's arm as he attempted to walk past her to get into the bathroom, so he could shower. It had been a few days. He not only needed to get clean, but the shower is where he took time out to clear his mind.

He allowed her to pull him by the arm until he was sitting on the bed next to her. Her small frame looked as if it disappeared next to his huge, muscular one. "What's good, baby?"

Jersey stroked his cheek with her thumb. "You tell me. I can tell there is something bothering you. We've been together way too long. So talk to me, let me know what it is."

Greed took a deep breath and exhaled. "We're being hunted, baby. For the first time, our family is being hunted and I'm not even entirely sure who it is that's comin' us. It's messing with my brain." He lowered his head and started to rub his temples with his forefingers, with a look of frustration.

Jersey felt somewhat afraid. Greed was the head. At the forefront of their family. She fed off his emotions. If he seemed like he had it altogether, he'd usually tell her that everything would be okay, and her mind would be at ease. But during the moments he seemed rattled, those were usually the times when their family went through a rollercoaster of chaos.

"Baby, do you have any idea whatsoever?"

Greed got up and started to pace back and forth with his shirt off. He looked like he worked out every single day. He had muscles on top muscles. He shook his head no. "Like I said before, I don't know of anyone I can say for sure one hundred percent, but I will do some digging."

The only name that kept coming to him was Money. For some reason, he just felt like it was him coming back to get at him. Back in the day, he had hit him for 20 kilos of cocaine and 60 thousand dollars. When the man had approached him about the caper, his teenage arrogance made him admit that he had taken it. Money thought it was in his best interest to threaten Greed in front of about 100 people over in Jamaica, Queens, but before he could get the threats fully out of his mouth, Greed beat him senselessly in front of all of them, and then again in Sing-Sing.

Money vowed whenever he got his weight up, he would kill Greed. Now that he was making major moves in the music industry, Greed felt he had enough financial backing to make good on his threats. He couldn't blame the man, but he was about to destroy anyone he thought had an affiliation with Money. In his mind, it was about to be a season of no mercy.

Jersey stood up and kissed him on the chest before rubbing him and looking into his eyes.

"I believe in you baby, and I know you're going to figure this thing out because you are a true street general. I'm riding with you until the end and I know you ain't gone let nobody take advantage of our family like that." She grabbed his face with both of her hands, making him look into her eyes. "Them muthafuckas nearly killed all of us. They shot our youngest baby and blew up the church with me, you and our oldest son in it. They must pay. It's your job to make sure they do. I believe in you. After you take your shower, you're gonna come back in here and fuck your wife. Then you're going to get our boys together and make some shit happen."

She reached into his boxers and squeezed his piece. "Do you hear me?" She knelt down, stroking his dick before kissing his big mushroom size head.

Greed felt her wrap her lips around him, sucking it hard. "Yeah, ma. You already know I do," he groaned as if he was out of breath.

Chapter 5

Greg pulled up to the red-bricked two-story house and put his car in park before turning off the ignition. It had been a long day. The house was the last call on his pizza delivery route before he could clock out. He yawned and stretched his arms above his head.

It was 10:30 at night and there was so much snow on the ground, nearly making it impossible for him to make it to his destination without slipping and sliding around like crazy.

He just wanted to deliver the last three pizzas, go home and get some sleep. He had to be right back up at 6 in the morning to pull another double at the restaurant. He was already exhausted but having a new baby in the house to support wasn't supposed to come easy.

He took off his seat belt and unlocked the back door before getting out of the driver's side and closing the door behind him. Reaching inside, he leaned down and scooped up the three pizzas, feeling the heat on the palms of his hands. To a normal person, they probably smelled good, but to him they reeked of just cheese. He was tired of the smell of pizza.

"I just wanna deliver these last fuckers and get home," he said out loud. "Uh!"

August crept up behind the man and grabbed a handful of his long, yet thinning hair. He yanked his head backward and exposed his neck before taking the heavily ridged hunting knife, slicing him from ear to ear. He watched the blood skeet across the interior of the car. It looked like the man's neck was a water sprinkler. He frowned and sliced it back and forth before pushing him into the Jetta, forcing him to the floor in the back. Wiping the knife on the man's clothes, he then took the pizzas and sat them on the passenger's seat. Then he got behind the wheel of the car and blew the horn excessively.

* * *

Banks heard the blowing of a horn outside and got irritated. He knew it couldn't be anyone except the pizza man but pulled the curtain back in the living room to confirm it anyway. Sure enough, there was a Davino's Pizza car out front. The driver sat behind the wheel as if he thought Banks was coming out in the cold just to grab the food when clearly it was his job.

"Baby, who is that blowing their horn out there?" Keisha asked, coming up behind him and rubbing his shoulders. They'd been married ever since their senior year of high school after Keisha got pregnant with their twins. Their relationship was intact though not always as strong as it could have been because Banks weakness for strippers.

"That's the pizza man. Dude bitch ass think I'm about to go out there in the cold and do his job, but he got me fucked all the way up. I'm finna let him know right now." He went and opened the door and immediately the wind attacked him. It was freezing outside.

"Pizza! Pizza! Pizza! Pizza! Pizza!" the little boys hollered again and again. Lyle and Lloyd were having a Power Rangers-themed sleepover for their eighth birthday. Neither could wait to get their hands on the pizza before the movie started.

Keisha put a finger to her mouth. "Shhhh! Y'all go back upstairs and quit making all that noise before I cancel the pizza. Now get! And keep yo' eyes on them boys up there. If something else comes up missing from my house, I'm gone lose it. I'm not kidding either."

Banks waved at the pizza man. "Aye, kid! You better bring that food to me. It's too cold! I ain't coming out there!" He threw his arms in the air.

August looked up at him and gave an evil smile. He opened the driver's side door, came around and picked up the pizzas, making his way up the walkway. The wind attacked him with a fury. His nose felt frozen and his lips were chapped. His cheeks felt like they had been on ice for three days straight.

Banks smiled. "I told you I was finna make this nigga fall in line. Didn't I, baby?" he joked to his wife.

She placed her hand on her wide hip and nodded. "You always do. That's why I love yo' ass."

Banks looked her up and down, feeling his dick hardened. For as long as they had been   together, she always turned him on like crazy. She had the body of a goddess in his mind and after their sons, she'd gotten even thicker. He thought about fucking her from the back right then and there. He would have to hit that ass, too. *That is definitely happening,* he thought to himself.

Keisha watched the yellow-faced pizza man bring their food to the door. "That'll be $31.97, please." She watched Banks turn around and frown. She heard the boys upstairs arguing. It sounded like they were seconds away from getting into a fight. That was the only thing wrong with having twins in her opinion was that they fought so much. She heard a loud smacking sound, turning and running up the stairs. "I know y'all not up there fighting!"

August took the distraction to handle business. He whipped the knife from his hip and quickly stabbed Banks twice in his shoulder blade, making him fall on to his stomach. He stepped into the house and looked toward the stairs where Keisha had disappeared to.

Banks felt the blade go into his back, crashing into his shoulder bones. It caused his head to snap backward before the pain shot all through him. His back locked completely up to the point he couldn't move. He first thought they were being attacked by the because he had made him bring the food to him. He felt helpless and he wanted to scream.

August wrapped his arm around him as if he were putting him in a head lock. "You're Money's right-hand man, right?" He pulled him in all the way and watched his brother Aiden step into the house behind him along with Greed.

As soon as Banks saw Greed's face, he started to panic. He knew that Money and Greed had a long-standing beef. Rumor had it that Greed was behind Money getting shot.

"Yeah man, but I ain't got shit to do with his beef between you and him. Greed, you know I ain't never disrespected you, cuz."

Greed leaned down and punched him so hard in the mouth, he knocked three of his teeth out. "Bitch nigga, I done heard my name in a few of yo' tracks on some disrespectful shit."

Aiden crept up the stairs listening closely to the commotion. It sounded like Keisha was   disciplining the children for fighting. As he got to the top of the stairs, he looked down the long hallway and saw that they were in the room furthest away. He dropped to his stomach and started to low crawl towards them with his knife in his mouth.

Keisha stood with her back towards the hallway, snapping. "Now, don't think just because y'all got company that I won't whoop y'alls asses all up and through here. Y'all ain't got no business fighting. You two are brothers. Y'all been begging me and your father for this party   ever since he got back off tour. Then you get it, and this is how we're repaid? I can't believe this shit. I mean, you don—" Keisha said before she felt something slam into her neck so hard, it felt like she was swallowing a block of wood.

Then as it was pulled back, she could feel it slice off a piece of her tongue and vocal cord. The world got dark and she felt herself falling backward as all the little boys hollered in terror. Aiden slammed the knife into her neck from the side. He was tired of her loud ass mouth. She had been talking ever since he came up the stairs. In his opinion, that was the worst thing about women. They simply talked way too damn much at times. It was annoying. He ripped her throat apart before slamming her head against the side of the door so hard, it split open like a pumpkin.

After she fell backwards, he threw her out of the way and closed the door behind him. There were about eight little boys and all of them were hollering at the top of their lungs, crying real tears. He smiled and grabbed the one closest to him, a white boy with glasses. He picked him up by the throat and slammed the big knife into his chest twenty quick times before dropping him back to the floor. He then picked up his brother, doing him the same way. The second little boy fell on top of his brother, bleeding internally. Lloyd tried to crawl under the bed, so Aiden knelt and stabbed him over fifty times in the back, shredding him apart before pulling his leg and throwing his dead body on top of the other two.

"Please don't kill me, mister. I'm so sorry. I won't fight my brother anymore!" the other twin whimpered.

Aiden turned his head to the side and looked him over closely. He saw his little tears rolling down his cheeks and his nose running. He looked so sad and vulnerable. Aiden frowned. He took him and the other fat boy that stood on the side of him crying, banging their heads together   repeatedly until the room was filled with their blood and shattered skulls. After he dropped them, he slit the throats of the other three boys, letting them off easy. He was bored and over the entire scene already.

August took the blade and ran it deeply across Banks' cheek so deep, the blade sunk into his face and hit his cheek bone before getting stuck. He yanked the knife out and stood behind Greed.

Banks felt the blade tearing open his face. It felt like somebody was burning him with fire on his right side. It hurt so bad he screamed like a girl at the movies watching a scary picture.

"Arrrrrgh!"

Greed punched him right in the eye so hard, he

shattered his socket causing the left side of his face to cave in. He saw a bright blue light, then felt dizzy. Greed smacked him awake.

"Nigga, tell me why ya man's tried to kill my whole family? This beef shit was between me and him."

Banks entire left side of his face felt like it was shutting down. The pain shooting from his eye socket was intense. It made his eardrums ring. He took a deep breath and bit into his lip to keep from hollering out in agony.

"Yo, Sun. That shit ain't got nothing to do wit' me, man. I don't know what that nigga Money finna do before he do it. He don't tell me shit. All we do is rap together, Greed. You know I ain't never been no street nigga. I'm 'bout this family life, man."

Greed frowned and slapped him with the back of his hand, causing him to fly out of the chair. "I hate when you tough niggas get to acting like hoes once the heat is on." He wiped his mouth with his leather gloved hands. "Pick his punk ass up and sit him back down," he ordered August.

August grabbed him by the throat and picked him up into the air, looking him over before he curled his lip in disgust. He slammed him back into the chair.

"All that tough shit and this is yo' true nature right here. You make me sick," he spat. He couldn't wait until he was given the order to body him.

Greed stepped to the side of the man, balled his fist and swung with all his might, directing his punch at the side of Banks's nose. He wanted to break it off his face.

Banks felt the blow, then heard his nose snap so

loud, it sounded like a firecracker to him. The pain shot all the way up to his brain, then into his eyes before he started hollering as if someone was killing him.

Greed looked him over. His nose was bent all the way to the right of his cheek with so much blood coming out of the nostrils, Greed knew it wouldn't be much longer before he passed out from the loss.

"Nigga, tell me what I need to know, or I'm gone have my nephew cut yo' ass up until he get tired. And let me tell you, this lil nigga is just like me. He lives for this murder shit, so he ain't gone never get tired. Why the fuck that nigga Money clapping at my whole family? Bitch nigga tried to kill us in a church yesterday at my people's funeral. So that mean all families are now in play. Tell me what the fuck I wanna know or I'm bodying you and yours tonight," Greed said, looking up in time to see Aiden coming down the stairs with blood all over him. He looked like a yellow ass Jason Voorhees.

Banks really didn't know shit about the hit on Greed's life, but he was going tell him whatever he thought to spare him and his family's life. The truth was Money didn't even fuck with him like that anymore ever since a few of his albums flopped. He considered him dead weight. Even him and Yayo hadn't been in contact with him in nearly a year.

"Greed, him and that nigga Yayo been talking about coming at you, kid. Ever since that nigga Yayo got out, he been screamin' street justice on behalf of Money. They like two peas in a pod. That nigga will do anything he say do. It's always been like that. That fool got a crib over in Brooklyn. I'll give you the address and everything. If shit got set up, the brains behind   everything is definitely Yayo. That bitch nigga grimy." He closed his eyes as a wave of dizziness came over him. It made him want to throw up.

Greed looked down on him with disgust. One thing he hated was a nigga that rolled over on his homies when the heat was on. It made him sick to his stomach. So after he made him give up the address to Yayo's crib, he gave the order to August to execute him.

August smiled, and took the opportunity to show off in front of Greed and his older brother Aiden. He swung the big knife forward with all his might, forcing it into Banks' face. He   immediately ripped it to the left and right, then pulled it out and slammed it into his neck once, then two times, then three times. Greed knew it he was going berserk, watching his tongue hang out as he stabbed him over and over again until he lay in the chair with his eyes wide open. His face looked like an angry bear had attacked it.

Banks felt the first stab enter his face. The blade landed right under his right eye and got stuck, causing his eye to blink repeatedly on its own accord. Then he felt the blade getting pulled out of his face, literally hearing the saw in his ears as it exited, only to be slammed into his neck. The point broke the skin, feeling like a lion had taken a bite out of him. The blood ran down his shoulder and dripped down to his stomach before the blade entered his neck again.

He screamed in his head. He begged for mercy.

His vision was of a man swinging back and forth, attacking him. The lights got dimmer and he got dizzy. Then he saw an Angel welcoming him, trying to pull him out of his physical body to help him escape to a place where there would be no pain or discomfort. He saw himself reaching upward, trying to grab the hand but then Greed appeared. He looked directly into his face, turning his head sideways before taking his Tims and slamming them into his chest, stopping his heart from beating indefinitely.

Greed kicked him out of the chair and looked down on him with hatred. Nobody was going to attack his family and get away with it. Nobody. He couldn't wait to pay Yayo a visit. He wanted to take the drama straight to Money, but he knew the man was out of the country touring with SZA. He wasn't due to be back into the states until later next week. It was all over social media.

Chapter 6

"Daddy, you mean to tell me that you flew me all the way out here just so you could get some of this pussy" China asked, slowly slipping out of her Yves St. Laurent body suit. She was thick as they came. Jazzy, a mixed Asian and black, stood at 5'4" and weighed 130 pounds. She was Chicago born and bred and was all about her paper.

King sat back on the bed and pulled off his boxers. "I wanna fuck that pussy. You always talking about me fucking other hoez when I'm on the road handling business. Now I fly you out here first class just so I can get me some of that body and you acting like it's a problem. What's really good?"

China slipped two fingers into her Yves St. Laurent panties and separated her sex lips before sliding a middle finger deep into her center. Her pussy was already hot and wet. She felt her walls trying to suck in her digit. She slowly made her way over to the bed.

"N'all daddy, I ain't saying it like that. I'm just surprised. That's all." She knelt in front of him and pulled on his long dick. Stroking it up and down, she squeezed and felt the thickness in her hand. That was one of the many things that she loved about King. His dick was huge and he knew how to use it. He'd taken her virginity when she was only 16 years old while they were on a trip to Hawaii he had paid for. Ever since that day, she'd been addicted to big dicks although his was the only one that had ever been inside of her. She pulled the skin back and sucked on the head loudly.

King groaned deep within his throat. His baby momma gave the best brain ever in his opinion. But having the kind of money he had allowed him to run across all types of females that had different styles when it came to sucking dick. Still China was rawer than all of them to him. He loved how she always pulled his skin all the way back, focusing strictly on the head. To him, that was the most important part.

China sucked as hard as her jaws would allow her to. She took her tongue and ran it up and down his pee hole, stroking his dick up and down. The noises she made drove him crazy. She meant to make them and knew that it was a part of the process. Whenever she sucked him the right way, he always fucked her into a coma damn near.

King reached over her back and smacked her ass before rubbing the thick globes. Her panties were stuck all in the middle of her creases.

"Open yo' knees, China so daddy can see that pussy pop out." It wasn't nothing like seeing a woman's pussy through her panties. To King, it was the hottest thing in the world and China's pussy was pudgy. It looked like she had four sets of lips because her inner lips hung slightly passed her outer ones. Then he knew from experience that her shit was good.

China spread her knees and heard him groan before rubbing his fingers into her crease. She felt the panties trap themselves between her sex lips and her ass hole. It turned her on like crazy.

"Umm, Daddy. Let yo' baby suck this dick real good. Just keep playing wit' me."

Her long hair fanned out around his thighs as her head went up and down, sucking him like a true champion. The noises got louder and her lips got tighter. She got to stroking him so fast that his toes curled. He started humping in her mouth at full speed while she squeezed his dick like she was mad at it. King felt his nut coming from all over his body.

He started imagining himself fucking her in the ass while she screamed at the top of her lungs until he couldn't take it anymore. He wanted to tell her that he loved her. He wanted to tell her how much he appreciated her, but then his "G" kicked in and he wasn't down to do none of that. He growled and got to bussing all into her mouth.

China felt the hot strings hit the top of her mouth and she smiled. His juice tasted like hot, salty cream. She milked his dick, stroking it up and down, forcing the nut to ooze from the top of it. Then she licked it away as if it were frosting. King got up and threw China on the bed, forcing her to spread her thighs all the way apart. As soon as they were as far as they could go, he leaned in and sucked up her lips, tasting her juices that were all over them. Taking three fingers, he slowly eased them inside of her back and forth, sucking on her clitoris.

China forced his face deeper into her. He was driving her crazy. Her clit was extremely   sensitive. She could barely take it. His fingers running in and out of her. His hot breath. His thick lips. She knew that she was getting the dick next. It was all too much. She arched her back, after wrapping her thick thighs around his head and screamed. "Ahhhhhh sheeeeit, dadddyyy! Here it cooommmmeeesss!"

Her orgasms rocked her like an earthquake. She felt it coming from all over her body. The shaking was intense. She pulled on her nipples and twisted them. King felt her skeeting into his mouth again and again. It made his dick hard. His baby mother tasted salty and sweet at the same time. Her thighs tightened around his head and he struggled breathing, but he kept on sucking her clit until she started shaking so bad that she released him.

He got up and flipped her on her back, pushing her knees to her chest. He busted her pussy wide open before taking his dick and sliding it inside of her thick ass body. The pussy felt hot and meaty. It seared him, causing his to close his eyes. China ripped her own bra off and exposed her C-cup titty. Her nipples were super hard. Her areola covered nearly the entire titty. Her nipples stood out a cool inch from the discs.

"Fuck me, King. Please, daddy. Fuck yo' baby into this bed and make me squirt all over this big dick. Own this pussy!"

King closed his eyes and started to fuck her so hard, it hurt his abs from slamming forward so hard. He was trying to kill it and China loved every minute of it.

Her titties bounced up and down on her frame and her thighs jiggled like crazy. She could feel her pussy juices pouring into her asshole, drenching it. She took her arm and dropped it to her side before taking two fingers and putting them into her ass while King fucked her pussy like he hated her.

* * *

Averie was sitting on Rayjon's lap in living room of her new townhouse when Ajani entered the room. Her first mind told her to jump off his lap, so that's exactly what she did. She stood in the middle of the floor looking like a little girl that had just been caught screwing in her mother's house. She felt awkward and a little uneasy. Rayjon looked up at her like she had lost her mind.

"What's good wit' you, Averie?" he asked, dusting his Gucci jeans off.

Ajani laughed. "She must have forgot that I already know about y'all or something. You know how old habits die hard."

He took the blunt and lit it at the tip. "Shorty, I don't fuck wit' you on that level no more. You belong to bro. I ain't got time for all that cuffing a bitch shit. Our family in danger. The last thing I'm trying to be worried about is your feelings, nah mean?"

Averie lowered her head and felt like shit. There she was caught between two brothers. One was her ex and the father of her deceased son. The other was the true love of her life. A man that went to bat for her, making sure she was straight on all levels. She would die for Rayjon in a heartbeat. Ajani, on the other hand, she didn't know what to say about him.

Rayjon stood up and put his arm around Averie's shoulders just as the first tears left out of her eyes. "Yo, you good, lil' ma?"

He had a heavy heart for her. He knew she still had to be going through it with the loss of her son being so fresh. Averie was an extremely fragile woman. She needed a man that would stand beside her and hold her up at all times.

She lowered her head and shook it. "N'all, I'm not okay. I want to talk to Ajani, if you don't mind. I think me and him need to get an understanding. That will be the only way I'll be able to fully release him from my system." She turned to him. "Can me and you please go back here and talk?" She couldn't even make eye contact with him. She felt too weak and afraid.

Ajani frowned. "Yo, we ain't gotta talk about shit, shorty. Y'all good. Word is bond. My brother came and hollered at me like a man. I respect his gangsta and the love he got for you   because I been let that go. I need me a stripper bitch that like to fuck in all kinds of positions. She gotta be about that life. I can't have the same one. I need variety. Word is bond. Had he not stepped up to the plate shorty, I was finna leave you out in the cold. I'm just on some self-ish me focused shit right now." He took a strong pull from the blunt and inhaled deeply.

Averie blinked tears. She felt like she wanted to die. *How could a man talk to a woman like that when she had given birth to his child and nearly died in the process? How could he think so little of her,* she wondered to herself. She felt like trash and at the same time, angrier than a bear woken up out of its hibernation.

"Ajani, after all of the times I done stood by you, you can at least grant me a few moments of your time. Now, lets go back here to this muthafucking room and get an understanding! Now!" she demanded, walking past him and bumping the shit out of him.

He cocked back his arm and swung it forward ready to connect with her jaw when Rayjon locked his arm into his, pulling him backwards. In the process, Ajani dropped his blunt on the carpet.

"Bro, you betta get that bitch. On my word, I'll go stomp a mud hole in her, kid. You know me," he spat, mugging the shit out of the back of Averie's head.

Rayjon pulled him in, embracing and cuffing his head like he used to do him when they were kids. "Chill, bro. You're better than that. We ain't gotta put our hands on a female to get an understanding. I want you to go back there and y'all squash this shit so we can move on with life. You my little brother, man. I don't love nobody more than you. Nobody. You got that?" He kissed him on the forehead.

Ajani's chest rose and fell. He was angry. He would have killed Averie in that moment had Rayjon not stepped in and calmed him down. He slowly started to nod his head. "A'ight, bro. Yo, I love you too, kid. And on the strength of you, I'ma squash this shit, but you better tell her to watch her mouth and respect my gangsta."

Averie rolled her eyes and looked at the ceiling. She hated how he was always telling somebody to respect him in some sort of way, but he was the most disrespectful person that she had ever met.

Rayjon made eye contact with her, almost scolding her. Without words, he'd told her to check herself and to fall in line so they could get past this. She nodded and lowered her head, walking all the way to the back room.

As soon as the door was closed, Ajani walked in

her face and grabbed her by the jaw with one hand. "Bitch, don't you ever flex on me like that. Now, I don't give a fuck about what you and my brother got going on, but if you ever come at me sideways like that again. I'm gone blow yo' head off. That's on my son." He rebuked, pushing her backwards.

She landed on the bed and curled into a ball, breaking down crying. Her heart was broken. *Why did he have to bring up their child in that manner?* she wondered. To swear by him that he would kill her was sadistic. It was low and she didn't understand why he was the way he was to her.

"Fuck you wanna talk about, man? I ain't got all day."

He adjusted the sleeves on his Pelle Pelle leather coat. His vest felt hot on his chest. His wounds that were healing started to itch. Only three weeks had passed since the incident and he still felt a little weak.

Averie slowly sat up, wiping away her tears. She swallowed and looked up to him. "Ajani, why do you hate me so much? What have I ever done to you?" she whimpered.

He mugged her and shook his head. "You always crying. That shit gets annoying. Word is bond, emotional bitches just get on my nerves. I can't deal with all of that. I don't know what my brother see in you, but sooner or later he won't no more."

Snot dripped out of Averie's nose. She wiped it away and sniffled. Tears were falling out of her eyes like crazy now.

"So you hate me because I'm an emotional female?"

Ajani looked at the ceiling and exhaled. "Shorty,

listen. I don't hate you at all. I'm just done with you. I been over you for some time now. Everything gotta run its course. That's just the way life works." He zipped up his jacket. "Now, I'm happy for you and bro. I wish y'all the best and I hope that he sees in you what I never did. That fool love you. I can see that shit all in his face and that's crazy because Rayjon used to love different varieties of pussy more than me. So I'm definitely shocked." He shook his head. "You got a decent shot on you, an okay grade of pussy, but it ain't enough to make a mafucka settle down and fuck just you."

Averie could clearly see that she wasn't going to get anywhere with Ajani. She had to accept things for what they were and move on with her life. It was all that she could do. "Well, thank you for wishing us well. And I hope that he does see in me what you never did. I will be the best possible woman that I can be to your brother. I just want you to know that I will always love you for the sake of our son. There are no hard feelings, right?"

Ajani took his pistol out and cocked it back, before putting it on his waist. "Nah, shorty. We good. Life goes on. Just make sure the homie stay straight and I'm good." He opened his arms so she could get up from the bed and walk into them. Averie hesitated for a brief second. She didn't think that hugging him was appropriate, but she figured what the hell. It would be the last time they had to do anything like that, a mature releasing of one another. She walked into his open arms and he closed them, holding her tightly.

"Ain't nobody in this world perfect, baby. But

shit will figure itself out sooner or later." He kissed her on the forehead and that made her uncomfortable. "I don't want to see nothing bad happen to you, so be careful. After all, you're still my son's mother." He reached down and cuffed her ass, squeezing as he slid his fingers underneath to feel her hot pussy searing the cloth.

She tried to push him away, but he held her. "Stop, Ajani. What's the matter with you?" she asked, struggling against his body.

He gripped that ass and spread it, opening her up. She could feel the light breeze of air shoot up her gown, going directly to her sex parts. He pulled her panties to the side and rubbed over her naked lips. They were as thick as he remembered. He pushed her to the bed. "Bitch, I'm just playing. I just wanted to feel them mafuckas one last time." He zipped his coat all the way up.

"I'm bout to go fuck something fresh and barely legal. Later." He opened the door and left her lying in the middle of the bed in tears.

Rayjon came into the bedroom and found her that way. He crawled into the bed after having a long conversation with Greed about his next mission, consoling her as best he could. She told him everything that transpired and it pissed him off.

He felt like his woman had been violated. Had that happened with any other man, he would have knocked his head off as soon as he received the information. He felt disrespected that his little brother would do something like that. After all, he made it seem like he was cool with them being together. If that was the case, then it was time he honored every facet of their relationship all around the board.

He pulled Averie up and wrapped her into his embrace. "Baby, listen to me. Stop crying." He kissed her on the forehead and wiped her tears away. "Baby, I promise you on my life that I ain't honoring no shit like that no more. That's my little brother, but at the same time you are my woman. It's my job to protect you at all times against anybody, including my own family. So, I'm checking that shit. You hear me."

Averie heard his words and more tears fell out of her eyes. She couldn't believe that he was ready to take a stand for her. She couldn't believe that he saw her worthy of all the drama. She wanted to literally break down in his arms and melt into his soul, so they could become one.

"I asked you did you hear me, ma?"

She nodded her head before wrapping her arms all the way around him. Her body shook. She could barely control herself.

"Yes, baby. I hear you and thank you for standing up for me because you know you don't have to do any of this. I'm not really worth it." She blinked tears and her body started to shake again.

He held firmly, kissing her on the forehead. "You are worth more than just this. This is the least that any man can do for you. It's my job and I'm gone stand beside you happily and on my gangsta."

In response to that, Averie laid her head on his chest and cried her little heart out. Rayjon's top lip curled. The more she sobbed, the deeper he fell for her.

Chapter 7

Chris tooted up the thick line of cocaine and sat back on the couch pinching his nose. Cherry came over and sat on his lap. Out of the nine strip clubs that he owned, she was his head stripper and C.O.O. She was the first female that taught him the game and showed him how fast his money could add up if he stepped out into the sex industry.

First, it was just the two of them throwing small hotel parties with strippers from all over Chicago. At these parties, some of the top kingpins throughout the city would come and lean back for four hours straight and have some of the kinkiest sex with no questions asked. His girls catered to the men's fetishes and because they got down like that, Chris's paper was way up. By the time he and King ventured out into the heroin market, Chris was already hood rich.

Cherry sat on his lap and ran her hand over his deep waves before kissing him on the cheek. "I missed you, baby. These hoes been getting on my nerves in this mafucka. I thought I was gone have to whoop some ass."

They were in his main office with the door closed, yet you could still hear the music in the club booming. It was a Saturday night and the club was packed. "But you handled that shit, right? I mean didn't no chaos ensue in my establishment, right?"

She smiled and wrapped her other leg all the way over him, facing him. Kissing his lips, she said, "Baby, you already know I held you down. That's the reason you put me in charge, right?"

He reached around and gripped that big ass

booty. Cherry was high yellow with a few   freckles that peppered her face. Her hair was cut into a short Keri Hilson type style and colored red. She was slim thick. Meaning little up top, but once you got to her waist, her hips curved outward and she had a big, ghetto booty and thighs thicker than a choke sandwich.

Chris nodded. "That's exactly the reason why I left you in charge. Now, lets talk about my money. What you rake in the four days I was gone?"

She scooted back and got off his lap. She walked to the front of the office and pulled down the blinds before locking the door. Taking a few steps, she knelt in front of the mini refrigerator and moved it out of the way along with the carpet that it sat on. Then she started typing in the code on the digital secured-lock safe.

Chris straightened the cuffs on his shirt, fixing one of the buttons. He was rocking a Tom Ford business suit that was trending on Wall Street. He looked the part of a well-dressed business man but underneath was a pure street bred goon. Cherry reached into the safe and pulled out the four stacks of money, placing them on his desk.

"That's fifty gees right there. It would have been more than that, but we got a little   competition from that new Jamaican club up the street. Them bitches running around in that   mafucka butt ass naked and strapped. You already know how they be looking with clothes on, so imagine what they look like naked?" Cherry said, eyeing him closely. She was trying to get a rise out of him because she felt like the Jamaicans were impeding on their turf.

She wanted him to give the order to have them wiped out. That way they could get their chips all the way up to where they used to be. "Then the owner, some nigga from Kingston,   Jamaica, came through here the other day with about ten females and bought out the whole V.I.P. section. Word got back to me they were trying to come at all our girls. That shit ain't cool. Them mafuckas ain't got no respect."

Chris frowned. "Some nigga from Jamaica? What's his name?"

Cherry exhaled loudly. "They call him Heinous. From what I'm told, he was something like a prince to the streets back in Kingston, well respected. And he got a body count just as high as you and King's. They say he eventually gone wind up taking over this club too and the streets of Chicago. That nigga want you and King's throne."

Chris stood up. He fixed his suit coat and adjusted his Tom Ford tie with a devilish grin. "You already know ain't shit like that about to happen. Don't let this mafucking suit fool you. I'm still 'bout that life. Me and the homie just handling some business out east. After we take care of that, we gone move them punk mafuckas around. Until then, you boost up our promotions and get my business up in this district. Let them hoez know that anybody I catch colluding with them Jamaican mafuckas gone be flagged as disloyal. And I'm severing their contracts after disciplining they ass in my own way. This shit ain't a game."

Cherry smiled to herself. "Okay, daddy. Is there anything else you want me to do?"

Chris unzipped his pants and spread his legs

apart, then pulled out his dick. "Do I even have to ask?"

Cherry licked her lips, and damn near broke her neck falling to her knees before him.

* * *

Ajani beat on the door again and rang the doorbell to his aunt's two-story house. He was about to start beating it like a man that had lost his mind when he saw the curtains move   backward on the other side and then the door opened.

"Boy, what the fuck you doin' beatin' on my door like you done lost yo' damn mind? I'm in here sleep. I gotta work tonight." She yawned, covering her mouth.

Ajani looked at his Rolex and noted that it was forty-five minutes after two. He gave her a look like she must have been crazy. He bumped the door open, walking inside. "Aunty, it's late in the afternoon. You better stop playing wit' me. I need to holler at you."

Vanity felt the door bump her forehead, taking a step back. She wanted to curse his ass out right then and there but decided against it. She knew her nephew didn't have it all. He had a   nasty temper just like her brother, Greed.

"About what, Ajani?" She tightened her Gucci robe around her body and looked up the stairs towards her bedroom. Her fiancé was up there in bed sleeping. They had just made up after   having a long argument over finances. The last thing she needed was for him to get up and get into it with Ajani. She just didn't know how that would play out.

Ajani walked over and pulled her into him roughly. "First of all, you can quit acting like you got some kind of attitude with me. I came all the way over here, so I could seek your advice and you treating me like one of them punk ass tricks in yo' club. This ain't that." He looked down on her and frowned.

She tried to push herself away from him, but he had a firm hold on her. "Okay, baby. Then just tell me what's going on."

"First of all, I missed you." He reached around and gripped her booty, rubbing all around it, not feeling any panty line which told him that she was nude underneath.

He squeezed that big booty and pulled the cheeks apart before sliding his fingers under her globes, rubbing her pussy from the back. It felt hot as a sauna and his dick got hard immediately. He leaned in and sucked on her caramel neck.

Vanity closed her eyes and allowed for him to do what he wanted for a few moments before she snapped out of it, remembering her fiancé was upstairs. She tried to push him away.

"Ajani, you gotta stop, baby. Trevor upstairs and I ain't trying to get caught fucking around like this. That man is crazy. You already know that. Uh, baby."

Ajani pulled her gown up slowly until it was sitting at the small of her back over her ass. He took his fingers and slid them into her pussy from the back and slowly worked them in and out of her, sucking on her neck like a Vampire.

"You know I don't give a fuck about that nigga,"

he said, his fingers fucking her slowly in and out, in and out, in and out. He pulled them out of her pussy and sucked them clean. She   tasted forbidden. It was taboo, that good shit.

Vanity stood on her tippy toes and arched her back as she felt him slide them back into her wet opening. "Nephew, you gotta chill. You can't be coming over here and doing this to me. This ain't right. I'm about to get married. You gotta respect my man now."

Ajani picked her up and slammed her against the wall, biting into her neck so hard that she kicked the lamp off the table in the front room. He held her up by her thick ass, licking the small trace of blood from her neck. He could feel her wet pussy against his stomach.

"Like I said before, fuck that nigga. If I want this pussy, then I'm gone come and get me some. I don't care if it's y'all wedding night, I'm still coming to get me some. Even if I gotta take this shit." He ripped open her gown at the top and her brown titties popped out, her nipples heavily engorged.

"Uhh, shit!" A bolt of sexual electricity shot through her and wound up shocking her clit.

The way he manhandled her and talked that shit in her ear drove her crazy. Her nephew did something to her that she couldn't explain. She was ashamed of herself and didn't give a fuck at the same time. Ajani lowered his pants and popped his dick through his boxer hole. As soon as it popped out, he bit into her neck.

"Put my dick in that pussy right now, Aunty. I ain't playing either. I want you to put this big dick in you and you finna let me fuck you like that nigga up-stairs can't. You already know how I get down. Now do it!" He crashed her into the wall hard.

Vanity had pussy juices running out of her as if she was peeing. Her nipples were so hard, they hurt her. She felt his huge dick head up against her hole, wanting to devour him. Nobody had ever fucked her the way that he had. Damn the fact of who he was to her. None of that shit mattered when he was deep in her stomach.

"Do it, now!"

"Vanity! Baby, what's going on down there?" Trevor hollered from up the stairs.

"Put my dick in you now or I'm finna go up there and kill homeboy."

"Trevor, I'm on my way up there, baby. Every-thing down here is good." She gripped Ajani's huge dick and put the head in her hole, feeling him slam her down. His dick shot into her body and hit the bottom of her stomach. It felt so good, she came imme-diately. "Uhhh, sheeeitttt!"

Ajani frowned and slammed her down, then brought her all the way up, pounding her out like a savage. "This my pussy, Aunty. This my shit. I'm fucking you whenever I want to. Tell me I can." He slammed her down harder, forcing her to take him deeper. Her pussy was so hot and wet, it felt swampy. He could feel her juices running down his dick and getting mingled with his pubic hairs that were under his balls. *Forbidden pussy was the best*, he thought.

Vanity closed her eyes and bounced up and down on him like a little girl riding a horse. She felt him beating her walls loose and it felt like heaven. She dug her nails into his shoulders and kissed his lips, sucking all over them full of lust. His big dick was opening her up wide. She could feel a little pain and it made it that much sweeter.

"Fuck me, baby. You can fuck me whenever you want to. This yo' pussy. It's yo' pussy baby. Just cum in me. Please bust that nut deep in my belly."

Ajani fell to the floor with her and really got to long stroking her with his eyes closed. That pussy was super good. The sound of her wetness as he continued to beat down her walls, was like music to his ears. Her walls milked him, and he couldn't hold back anymore. He had to buss in her. He had to cum in her as deep as he could. He hurried and threw her right thigh on his shoulder and choked her with his right hand, fucking her like an angry beast.

Vanity felt him attacking her and all she could do was close her eyes as tears slowly slid down her cheeks. The dick was so good, and he was pounding her into the floor like an animal. Every spot that needed to be hit was hit. Every itch that needed to be scratched, he scratched. He fucked the living daylights out of her so much, that she passed out.

When she woke up, she was bent over the couch. She felt him fingering her ass before sliding his dick slowly into her. By the time she thought about protesting, he was hitting her, and she was bouncing back into him with her titties flopping underneath her.

* * *

King waited until Rachael got into her car before

walking up to the driver's side door and knocking on the window. He had been watching her for the last three hours, waiting for an opportunity to get close to her. After she went through the drive thru of McDonald's, he'd thought about running up beside her car and airing her out, then jumping back on his Ducati and pulling away. He knew that she was Jersey's younger sister. Her death would shatter their family. He felt like a cat that played with a mouse before it eventually killed it. He was going to play with the Edwards family before he wiped them all off the face of the earth.

Rachael heard the knock and looked up. She saw a fine, brown-skinned man who looked like Idris Elda. She licked her lips, already having visions of him being her baby's father. She wondered why he was knocking on her window. She placed the hot bag of food in the passenger's seat and rolled down her window.

"Uh, yeah. May I help you?"

King smiled and licked his thick lips. "Yeah, ma. See, I'm new around here and I found myself lost. I'm trying to find Washington Park because my lil' niece is having her birthday party there. I promised I'd help set up, so I know my sister probably mad at me right now," he lied, licking his lips enough to entice her.

King knew he was a fine man. More than enough females told him that ever since he was a young boy. For some reason, most were obsessed with his lips, so he played that card often.

Rachael batted her eyelashes and smiled. "Well, all you gotta do is call one of them and they should

69

be able to give you directions. That seems simple enough."

She raised an eyebrow at him, not buying the lie he was selling. The year was 2017. It was damn near 2018 and all he had to really do was type in the location he wanted to find on his phone and the information would be provided for him. She felt he could have come up with   better game than that one.

King looked into her beautiful face and smiled. "Damn, so you gone just catch me up like that, huh?" He shook his head and looked around. He wanted to pop her in the forehead and keep it moving, but there were way too many people around for that and he was unmasked. He took a deep breath and exhaled slowly. "A'ight, let me get off this bullshit. I peeped you from a   distance and even though I couldn't really see was your face, I thought you looked real good, obviously good enough for me to come over here and make a fool of myself. So now that I did, I guess I need to ask you if that killed my chances of getting your number?"

Rachael shook her head. "I knew you was lying. I hope you don't play poker because I saw right through that shit. But you good. Let me grab my phone."

She reached in the backseat of her Mercedes Benz Roadster to retrieve her phone. As soon as she wrapped her hand around it, she heard the driver's door opening. King scanned the entire   area as she reached into the backseat. Thankfully the snow started to fall again. It came down like a white blanket with the sun going down behind the clouds, causing the streets to become dark. He used this help from

Mother Nature to benefit his mission.

As soon as he saw her reach backwards, he pulled open the door and got in, sitting on top of her. Rachael started to punch him in the back of the head again and again. Her face was balled up, her heart beating faster than an African drummer. She should have known the man had more on his mind than her number. Their family was under attack. Jersey had told her this more than a hundred times over the last few days.

Bam! Bam! Bam!

King elbowed her in the face three times. Her head jerked backward violently, yet she kept on fighting him, even from a state of dizziness. He felt her bite into the back of his head. It hurt so bad, he hollered out.

"Ahhh! You punk ass bitch!"

"Fuck you, muthafucka! You gone have to kill me, but I promise you it ain't gone be sweet." She reached around and punched him again and again in the face and jaw. The car rocked like somebody was on the hood jumping up and down.

King butted his head backwards and connected with her face, bussing her nose and mouth wide open. He could feel the blood squirting across his neck and head, dripping down into his jacket and down his back before sliding into the waistband of his pants.

Rachael felt his head smash into her face and everything went blurry. She felt dizzy, then the pain in her nose started. It felt like she had been hit in the face with a huge brick not once, but twice. Blood spurted out of her nose and mouth and dripped down to her chest. She felt him slam his head against hers again, then everything faded to black.

Thirty minutes later, she was jolted awake by the feel of something freezing cold on her face. Her eyes popped open and the same man was standing over her. She was on her back and could feel the frozen blood stuck to her face.

"What do you want from me? Why are you doing this?"

King straddled her weak body and pulled out his scalpel, holding her by the throat as he carved Greed's name in big letters. He dug real deep into her forehead. So much so that he was scraping against bone as he did his thing. Rachael felt the stinging on her forehead, screaming as loud as she could. It felt as if a million bees were stinging her all at once. The cool night's air attacked her face until the hot blood ran out of her wounds, warming her for the moment.

The weight of him on her chest made it hard for her to breathe. She couldn't understand why any of it was happening to her. She didn't get involved with what her sister's husband did. Yeah, it was true that she had allowed him to partially raise her sons because Aaron was such a dead beat. It was because of that, she'd lost her reigns on them. She knew they had many sins against them, but she loved them just the same. As for herself, she never indulged in what they did, so she couldn't understand why she was meeting this fate.

King looked down on her with hatred. "Your only downfall is being related to Greed. My mission is to wipe out his entire bloodline. And word is out that you're his sister. Therefore, bitch, you gotta go."

Chapter 8

King wrapped his hands around her neck and squeezed as tight as he could, his veins popping out of his neck. He could feel his muscles tensing up. He squeezed harder and harder, watching her eyes pop out of her head.

Rachael wanted to tell him she was Jersey's sister instead Greed's. In fact, Greed was her brother-in-law, not sharing any blood at all. That he was making a huge mistake and should reconsider his attack, but it was too late.

She felt him wrap his hands around her throat, then he got to squeezing. She heard her neck pop, cutting off her airway. It didn't help that it was freezing cold outside. That only made matters worse. She opened her eyes wide and started kicking her feet. She wanted to swallow but couldn't. She tried it again, but the spit she tried to swallow made it feel like she was being smothered with plastic. She started to panic, flopping around like a fish.

One lung collapsed, exploding like a big balloon causing her to bleed internally. She felt the blood rushing into her throat as he began to squeeze tighter and tighter. Her chest felt like it was under a parked car. King raised his fist and brought it down with all his might right into her chest.

Wham!

She jerked and inhaled a bunch of air just like he'd hoped she would. Then he started choking her like his life depended on it. Rachael couldn't breathe. Her second lung collapsed, and blood spilled out of her mouth. Her chest felt like she had swallowed a bag of nails. She kicked her feet as the world began to fade away.

She saw the faces of her children in her mind. She saw when they were just little boys falling over everything, trying to grasp the concept of walking. Then she saw their funerals. She saw the man that was killing her killing them. Her little babies. She loved them so much. She wanted to protect them, but she was being smothered. The world got dark as her heart exploded in her chest. It felt like an army tank had just shot her.

King felt her jerk one last time, then she was as limp as a wet noodle. Blood poured out of her mouth and ran down her neck in thick globs. He smiled. Before leaving, he used her blood to write the name "Greed" in big bold bloody letters on her forehead.

* * *

Ajani slammed into Vanity's ass as she held it open for him. Tears ran down her cheeks and her mouth was wide open, moaning brazenly. It felt so good she didn't know what to do other than diddle her jewel while he fucked her like crazy.

"What the fuck is going on down there?" Trevor yelled from the top of the stairs. He ran to his hall closet and retrieved his .45 automatic before running down the stairs pointing it at the couple who were struggling to get dressed.

Ajani eyed Trevor the whole time and smiled. He didn't think he had that "G" shit in him like that, so he wasn't worried about him using that pistol. As soon as he got his pants pulled up, he grabbed his gun from under the couch and cocked it back. It was an all-black Glock .40, seventeen shots of pure hell.

"Bro, don't even come at me with that dumb shit. This my Aunty. We family and hell yeah, I was fucking that ass. What, nigga?" He held his pistol at his side, ready to do whatever Trevor wanted to do.

Vanity ran in front of Trevor and tried to wrap her arms around the high yellow man who resembled Shemar Moore.

"Baby, it ain't nothing like that. My nephew just needed me and one thing led to another. I promise I ain't never cheated on you with no other man," she hollered.

Trevor pushed her away from him and smacked her so hard, she yelped. "Shut up, bitch! I ain't trying to hear none of that right now."

Trevor was an old pimp that gave the game up about ten years back after serving a bid in Attica. He wasn't one of those soft light-skinned niggas like most cats took him to be. He was about that life and he didn't have problem whooping a bitch or popping a nigga.

Ajani didn't get that message because as soon as Trevor smacked Vanity, he swung and smacked him upside the forehead with the Glock so hard, that it split him open. His gun flew across the floor and Ajani was on his ass like white on rice.

"Bitch nigga, you wanna put yo' hands on my Aunty. I'm finna beat you to death. Word is bond."

Trevor tried to get up, but Ajani whacked him again with his gun. The pain shot across his face, making him scream like a bitch. He fell on his back, then Ajani got on top of him. He brought the gun down against the side of his head not once or twice but three times, splitting it wide open. He had his mind set on killing him in cold blood. He hated bitch niggas like him. He felt he had no right to stop him from fucking his aunty. It wasn't his business. They were family and family ruled over everything else. That's the way the game went, period.

"Ajani, no! Stop it! You're killing him!" Vanity screamed, watching her nephew literally beat her fiancé's brains out.

She ran and jumped on his back, causing them to fall backwards. Ajani felt her damn near choking him, pissing him off.

How the fuck was she going against family, he asked himself. He peeled her hands from around him and tried to wiggle out of her grasp, but she jumped on him again. He could feel the pain from his old injuries coming to the surface, nearly knocking the wind out of him. He stood up and tried to shake her off him.

"Vanity, get the fuck off me. Let me handle this nigga. You know how we get down in this family."

Vanity cried. "I just don't want you to kill him, nephew. Please don't kill my man. I need him," she whimpered. They fell to the floor with her arms and legs wrapped around him.

Ajani though about using his pistol to knock her off him but decided against it. "Get off me, Vanity. I ain't gone tell you again." She had his back on fire.

Trevor slowly turned on his stomach and low crawled toward his pistol until he had it in his hand. Blood ran into his eyes, making it hard for him to see.

He could feel the air going into the huge gash on his forehead and on top of that, he felt crazily woozy. He grabbed the pistol and aimed with one eye open.

Vanity jumped off his back and started to beg him. "Please, just let me handle this, Ajani. Please, baby. I don't want anybody.to get hurt. Please."

Ajani looked up at her after falling from the ground. His back was killing him, making it hard for him to stand up. He was over it. If she wanted to stay in the house with an abusive ass, yellow nigga, then he was gone let her do that. It wasn't his problem.

"You know what, Vanity? Fuck this shit if you wanna protect him."

Vanity's heart was beating fast. She just wanted it to all be over. She leaned down to help Ajani get to his feet when all the sudden, she heard a loud noise and everything turned red. It felt like she had a horrible headache. Then she saw the floor getting closer and closer, before everything went dark.

Boom! Boom! Boom!

Ajani watched the first two bullets smack his aunt into the face, her whole head exploding, and jerking backward. Her brains flew out the back of her skull and landed against the wall.

She fell forward face first and landed with her ass in the air. The tears shot out of his eyes immediately. He turned to Trevor.

Boom! Boom! Boom! Boom!

"Ahhh! Bitch ass nigga!

"Boom! Boom! Boom!"

The bullets slammed into Trevor's chest knocking him backward. He flew into the China cabinet with his arms in the air. He dropped his pistol and fell on his face, writhing in pain. Ajani came and stood over him, emptying the clip of his Glock. Ten shots all to his face. The bullets ate away his mug and left him looking like a smashed tomato.

Ajani fell to his knees and broke out in tears. He crawled over to Vanity and picked her up, cradling her in his arms as if she were the love of his life.

* * *

"Here go another ten gees, too. Later on this week, I just want you to go shopping and get whatever you want because you deserve it. You hear me?" Rayjon said to Averie before he kissed her on the lips.

He had just copped her a 2018 BMW truck. He felt that since she was now his woman he had to upgrade her on every level. It was cold outside and the streets were slippery. According to J.D. Power and Associates, BMW trucks were the best for those conditions, so the best is what he made sure she was rolling.

Averie sucked all over his lips, reaching through the window and rubbing his chest. Once she felt the bullet proof vest, she had butterflies in her stomach.

"Damn, baby. Do you still need to wear that?" She already knew the answer to the question. She just wished that it didn't have to be. She hated the lifestyle that he lived. Her ultimate goal was to get him away from it all.

Rayjon felt the wind pick up. "You already know what I'm up against out here in these streets. Right now, it ain't safe for any of us out here. That's why

I'm moving you down to Miami for a little while."

She felt like she couldn't breathe. He was trying to get rid of her. She felt that maybe he was tired of her. She started to panic.

"Baby, aren't you coming, too?" She whimpered afraid to hear his response.

Rayjon reached across her windshield and snatched the price tag of the truck's window. It was hers now bought, and paid for. He looked around at the lot full of trucks and cars. A few salesmen were doing their best to make a sale. He shrugged his shoulders and popped his collar.

"Look, I'm gone follow you down there, but first I gotta handle this business up here. I   wanna set you up an account that got about a hunnit gees in it. I want you to get shit together for me. That way when I get down there, there won't be much to do. Right now, my main focus is making sure you're straight."

Averie jumped out of the truck and wrapped her arms around him tightly. She blinked tears, feeling them come out of her eyes. She loved Rayjon with all that she was as a woman. He was her everything. He treated her like no other man ever had. She felt like she would rather die than leave his side.

"Baby, I know that you have my best interest at heart, but I can't be without you under no circum-stances. I would rather die with you then away from you any day." She broke down to her knees and put her face into her hands. "Don't you understand how much I need you. I can't live without you. You're my everything. I have never experienced the kind of love you render unto me. I don't understand it, but I don't want to lose it either. I'm not strong enough."

Rayjon fell to his knees in the snow and wrapped her into his arms. "Baby, I just gotta make sure that you're safe and sound because I love you. It's my job to protect you and keep you from harm. You are my woman and I think the world of you. There is nothing humanly possible that I would not do for you. My loyalty is real."

He squeezed her tighter and kissed her on the cheek just as the wind picked up, blowing the snow from the ground into their faces. The month of November was attacking them with a vengeance.

Averie looked up and kissed his lips. "I can't leave you, Rayjon. I just can't. So please don't make me."

* * *

Jersey ran past the yellow tape of the crime scene and pushed the police officer out of the way as he tried to block her path.

"Get the fuck out of my way, Blood. That's my sister over there."

He thought about preventing her from contaminating the crime scene, but thought better of it. He watched as she ran from him and dropped to her knees in front of the deceased. Jersey slowly peeled the sheet back and as soon as she saw Rachael's face with her eyes wide open, she threw up to the left of her. Wiping her mouth, she eyed her sister's corpse closely and noted the carving of her husband's street name on her forehead. Somebody was definitely trying to send them a message. She felt her heart break in two.

Out of all of her sisters, Rachael was her best friend and closest sibling. She loved her with all of her heart. She leaned over and kissed her cold cheek. She felt a hand on her shoulder. She looked up and saw August standing over her wearing a half mask. His eyes were glossy as if he he'd been crying. He'd been the one to contact her once he learned oh is mother's murder. Being her last born, he was more like her than his brother. He squeezed her shoulder lightly and walked away without saying a word.

* * *

Ajani stood up, looking down at his aunt with a broken heart. He didn't know what to think or do. He wished he could've kill Trevor all over again. The man had cost him the woman he loved second to his mother. He felt the tears rolling down his cheeks and fell back on his knees.

* * *

King took a step back and kicked the door right by the lock with all of his might, knocking it off of the hinges.

Whoooom!

As soon as it flew in, he upped his Mach .11 and cocked it. He knelt down and started going through the house with it against his shoulder as if he were a Navy Seal or something. Ajani heard the door being kicked in, nearly having a heart attack. He fell to his hands in a push up   position, trying to get back up but slipped on Vanity's blood, causing him to fall on to his back. The pain shot up and through him almost immediately. He struggled to get up, his pistol raised in the air.

King put the beam right on his forehead. "Bitch nigga, you move and I'm gonna blow yo' mutha-fuckin' head off." He wiggled his finger over the trigger, anxious to squeeze. He couldn't believe his luck if it was who he thought it was. He was pretty sure he had his beam planted on Greed's youngest son's forehead. If that was the case, then he had plans on making the biggest statement of all.

Ajani could feel his heart beating fast. It felt like he couldn't breathe. He was caught in the act slipping and there was nothing that he could do about it. He had visions of grabbing his gun off of the floor, turning, and shooting at the man. But with that beam on his forehead, all it would take was for him to squeeze that trigger and he knew his brains would've been knocked out of his head, so he frowned.

"What the fuck you kicking in my aunty door for, nigga? This shit ain't got nothing to do with you." He slowly stood up, refusing to put his hands in the air.

He squinted and smiled under his mask. "Oh, so you one of them tough ass niggas from out east, huh? You ain't gone go out like no bitch, is that it?" King took the beam and shined it from one of Ajani's eyes, then to the next.

Ajani sniffed and curled his upper lip. "I'm supposed to be scared because you got the ups on me, nigga?" He sucked his teeth loudly. "I been on the giving end before. Now, I'm on the other end. My old man always told me that when it was time to meet my Maker, take that shit like a man. So fuck you nigga and do what you gone do. Word is Bond. I don't bow down to nobody, only Jehovah."

King straightened his back up. He had to really look over the little muscle bound young man. He hoped that his son Prince would grow up to have the same amount of balls. He couldn't wait to meet Greed. If his son was this much of a killer, he could only imagine how looney his pops was. He trailed the beam down and shot him in each knee, shattering the kneecaps that covered them.

Chapter 9

Bocka! Bocka! Bocka! Bocka!

The bullets ripped into Ajani's kneecaps, shattering them immediately, then knocking them out the back of his legs. It felt like he'd been hit by a car head on. He actually heard the crunching before they popped into pieces. Then his legs bent inward. The pain was so horrible, he jumped into the air and came down hard on his chest, knocking the wind out of him.

"Arrrrgh, you bitch ass nigga!"

King sat his weapon down and walked over to him, grabbing him by the throat. He picked him up with two hands and carried him into the dining room where he slammed him on the   dining room table.

"You see, what you have to understand is that your father ain't the only muthafucking goon in the world. My name is King. I'm from Chicago, nigga, and what I'm finna do to you is what we do down there every day. Now, I been given the order to wipe out yo' bloodline and that's exactly what I'm finna do." He punched Ajani in the mouth, causing his head to bounce off of the table, then he picked him up and dumped him on his back.

Ajani felt the punch to his mouth. It felt like he had bitten into a slab of concrete. Then he was up in the air, corning down fast on his back. The old bullet wounds had him screaming out in pain. His knees were killing him, but all he could think about was Averie and how much he missed her. He wished he could kiss her one more time and apologize to her, telling her that he was really happy for her and Rayjon. He'd tell her how much he appreciated her for bringing their son into the world and that he wished he'd been there for her more when they lost him   because she deserved that comfort. He'd thank her and do his best to spoil her for all the times she had held him down while he was locked up. Then he would apologize for all of the cheating and the disrespect.

He missed her so much. He felt a tear sail down his cheek as King manhandled him. He'd just finished duct taping his hands over his head and his feet together. He then went into Ajani's pocket and pulled out his phone, strolling down the call log until he found the name "Pops". He knew it had to be Greed's number. As soon as he did, Greed picked up. King switched over to Facetime, sitting the phone up at an angle so he could see Ajani's body all laid out. He had   already removed his vest and shirt.

"Ajani! Ajani! What the fuck is going on, Sun?" Greed hollered into his phone.

"It's a wrap, Pops. This nigga name King say he finna wipe out our whole blood line. I guess I'm first. It's loyalty though, Pops. I ain't scared. I'ma take this shit like a man just like you taught me."

King laughed. He was finna see about that. He slid the scalpel out of its holster and straddled Ajani before stabbing it into the middle of his chest, slicing downward all the way to his pubic hairs. As he pulled the scalpel down, he scooted backwards until he was on the floor on his knees.

Ajani felt the stinging sensation of the blade cutting him open. It felt like he was being burned from the middle of his chest all the way to the top of his dick. When the blade ran over his belly button, it got stuck. King had to stab it harder, ripping apart the tough tissue that was there. It popped and then it split in two. The pain was unbearable. Ajani had tears coming out of his eyes.

Then he started thinking about his mother. He missed her beautiful face, especially her little freckles and how she would always cater to him, yet at the same time, keep him in his place. She was really the true definition of being a Queen.

King knelt down and put his eight fingers into Ajani's abdomen, pulling it wide open and ripping it apart. It was tough, but he did it with all of his might, grunting and doing all he could to accomplish the task. Blood shot up, splashing him across his mask. He could feel the hot liquid coating his fingers, making him smile.

Whenever he died, he hoped that he went out the same way because it was sadistic and worth talking about. He didn't want a boring death. Nah, that was weak to him. He felt that the little dude was a G, so he'd give him a death they would talk about for ages.

Ajani felt himself being ripped apart. He squeezed his eyelids together and tried to breathe. The pain was so horrible, he wanted to scream out like a woman in labor. He wanted Jersey. He wanted to see his brother Rayjon. He could hear the tearing of his skin and the beats of his heart getting louder and louder in his ear. Then there was a punch to his gut that knocked the wind out of him.

King punched his hand into the huge opening he'd created and felt around. He reached upward, the sounds of liquid and flesh heavy in his ears. It sounded like a washing machine after being opened with clothes tossing around inside of the water. He smelled raw like copper. King pulled his bloody hand out and grabbed the scalpel.

"Yo' son got a lot of heart, Greed. I gotta commend you on raising such a boy. I figured since you created that heart, you would want me to leave it behind for you."

King pulled on Ajani's large intestine and yanked it out little by little. It came out of his body like a long, pink and bloody rope. Ajani jerked upward with his eyes wide open. He could feel his insides being pulled out of him. It felt like his back was caving in. The pain was like the worst stabbing you could ever imagine. He wanted to die now. He longed for the fate of death. The pain was so horrible. It was too much for him to bear.

King saw the boy close his eyes. He reached and smacked him awake with his bloody glove. Ajani sat half way up before falling backwards. Blood poured out of his middle like an overfilled bathtub.

"Muthafucka, when I catch you I'm killing you, nigga! You wanna bring this shit to my family, bitch nigga. You and that nigga Money is dead."

Greed disconnected the feed. King chewed harder on his gum and hummed to himself as he carved Greed's name into Ajani's forehead, before standing up to admire his work. Ajani continued to jerk and shake on the floor. Blood poured out of his mouth, his eyes were now wide open. King knelt back down, reached into his middle, then upward and slightly to his right. He could feel the muscle that barely worked now.

The beats were slow and weak. He placed the back of his hand up against the heart, feeling it's heat before wrapping it into his hand. Then he pulled it out of his body enough to cut the artery that was attached to it. Blood spurted into the air. He squeezed the muscle harder, causing it to drip more of the fluid on to his Tims. He yanked on it and it came a loose. He opened Ajani's mouth and stuffed it in there.

When Ajani felt King reach into his body the last time, the light went out of his eyes. He felt his heart beating fast before the man pulled it from his chest. It felt like his spinal cord was folding in half, like somebody was stabbing him with a sword right in his chest. The pain was   horrible, then things started to get fuzzy.

His last thoughts were of seeing Averie in a wedding dress, looking fine as the day he'd met her in school. He tried to smile, but died before his face could form one. King put his phone into his pocket, looked down on the young man and nodded. He was pleased with himself.

"Now that's how you kill a bitch nigga, Chicago style!"

* * *

"Baby, that nigga Heinous just came into the club right now. He with all of them Jamaican bitches and they demanding to be seated in V.I.P., but we booked up to the gills. Ain't no room for all of them," Cherry said, looking over her shoulder back out into the club.

Chris pulled his dick out of Feature's mouth and yanked her up by her hair. "Bitch, go   downstairs and clean yourself up. You gone be going out on stage in twenty minutes and it's yo' job to make me proud. All your bills paid, right?"

She wiped her mouth and nodded, her beautiful caramel face lighting up. "Yes, Daddy."

"You rocking that new Audi A6, right?"

She nodded again, stepping back into her G-string. "Yes, Daddy."

Chris stood up and fixed his pants. "You see the way you smiling and beaming and all that shit? That's how I want my face to be when you step on and off that stage. We got some   muhfuckas in here that's gone be peeping yo' every move, so it's on you to represent me in the way that I expect you to. Don't let me down or I'm stripping yo' title, okay?" He reached into his desk drawer and threw her three gees, all one hundred dollar bills.

She caught it like a wide receiver with a big smile on her face. "I won't let you down, Daddy. You can believe that." She looked Cherry up and down before walking past her. Both girls locked eyes and turned their noses up, being jealous of each other.

Cherry frowned. "Bitch, you can leave."

Feature curled her top lip and rolled her eyes be-fore looking back at Chris, kissing her hand and blowing it at him. She smiled again and left his office through the tunnel that was built   inside of the wall. It led directly to the dressing room.

As soon as she left, Cherry mugged Chris filled with anger. "What the fuck was that all about?"

Chris straightened hid Ferragamo belt before

tucking in his Ferragamo shirt. "Shorty, don't bring that drama in here already. You know how I get down." He sat behind his desk and popped in a stick of Extra Spearmint gum, chewing loudly.

Cherry was heated. "I'm saying, why you gotta call that bitch in here? Now she gone think she all special and shit. She already looking at me all crazy like she on my level. Ugh." She crossed her arms in front of her and looked at the ceiling for no reason at all.

"That bitch turned 18 two days ago. That's fresh pussy. That's why she in my office. I gotta take advantage of her before she get all washed up and shit."

He placed the small mirror on his desk and poured a hefty sum of cocaine on to it. Then he took a baby spoon, scooping the coke up and treating his nostrils. The cocaine blasted him awake right away. He felt alert. He felt like he wanted to get on business or even splash something if he had to.

"So, what you saying? You saying I'm washed up. That just because that bitch young, she finna take my slot or something?"

She felt a little worried because she knew that in the stripping world, that the older you got, the less appealing you became. In the sex industry period, it was all about being young and fresh. After the age of 25, you were considered a vet or acquired taste, meaning that the only way you were sought after was if someone had a fetish for older women. That freaked her out because all the girls she had come into the game with were now full-fledged hoes. They had to sell pussy because the tricks in the clubs weren't really fucking with them. They tended to navigate towards the fresh pussy, women 17 to 21. Cherry was only 25, but she felt ancient.

Chris pinched his nose and swallowed. "N'all, I ain't saying you washed up. I'm just saying that she young and fresh, damn near jailbait. I wanna fuck on her until I get tired. Your slot straight. Now, tell me about this bitch ass nigga down there."

Cherry swallowed, damn near wanting to cry. She tried to get a hold of herself. She blinked and a tear sailed down her cheek. "Okay. Um, well his name is Heinous. He's from Kingston, Jamaica and he's supposed to be some type of legend over there." She wiped away her tears and took a deep breath, blowing it out slowly.

Chris looked her over with annoyance. "What the fuck is you crying for, Cherry?"

He frowned, wanting to send her out of his office. One thing he hated was a whiney or   crybaby ass female. He grew up as an only child. His parents were cold-hearted and didn't cater to feelings, so he was the same way. Crying got on his nerves. He hated when men did it when he tortured their ass and he hated when females did it whenever reality struck them in the face.

She shook her head. "I'm not crying. I'm just going through something right now," she said, wiping her face. She literally wanted to break down. She was an extremely emotional female, but she couldn't help it.

As annoying as it was to console her, Chris knew that he needed her because she was a beast when it came to keeping his clubs in order. She was only 25, but she had a knack for the game. He needed her as his right hand because King wasn't into the sex industry. He was a pure dope boy and hit man when the numbers were right. Chris needed Cherry because there wasn't a   species on earth that knew how to run a sex industry dominated by women more than a woman. So while he made it seem like her part wasn't that important, it really was.

"Baby, come over here and sit on Daddy's lap. I need you right quick."

Cherry lowered her head and slowly made her way over to him. She had butterflies in her stomach and before she could stop them, the tears were falling out of her eyes. She felt him pull her down by her waist until she was sitting on his lap.

Chris kissed her on the cheek. "Baby, you ain't got shit to worry about. As long as I'm breathing, you gone be straight for life. You know you be handling yo' business." He kissed her cheek. "Have I ever lied to you about anything as far as you know?"

Cherry shrugged her shoulders. "I don't know, but I don't think so. Most times, you're   brutally honest with me. Sometimes, too brutal." She lowered her head, then fell back and placed it on his shoulder. "Are you getting tired of my pussy? Like is it too old for you now?" She said these words barely above a whisper.

Chris didn't want to hurt her feelings, but the truth was that all pussy got old to him after a few fucks. He felt like there was way too many women in the world for a man to settle down and just fuck one pussy. He didn't think that a man was designed to get down like that.

Even all throughout the Bible, men had multiple

wives and concubines. Because of that, he felt that God knew man would get bored with just one hole. But he couldn't tell her that. If he did, he knew it would break her spirits. And when you had a woman running alongside of you handling business, you needed to cater to that emotional side of her or she would crumble mentally. So his job was to keep her mentally laced and empowered or all the tasks that he put her in charge of would fail.

"Baby, ain't none of them hoes fucking in yo' business. You're my baby and I got you for life. Them bitches here just to step in when I get bored or when I wanna try some shit, but you're my one. Don't forget that."

Cherry's heart melted. She felt like a million dollars all over again. She sat back and told him everything that she knew about Heinous, not leaving a single thing or tale out. As soon as she finished talking, there was a loud knocking on the door. Chris stood up, damn near pushing her on to the floor.

"Baby, see who that is."

He dusted off his pants, then rolled his head around on his neck. He figured the nigga   Heinous was going to be a problem for them. He sounded like he was super plugged and about that life. Chris and King had had a little experience dealing with Jamaicans and from what he   remembered, they truly were a problem.

Cherry looked back at him with a worried expression on her face.

"They say dude demanding V.I.P. and he wanna personally talk to you. What should I tell her to tell your security team?"

Chris mugged her as if everything that was taking place was her fault.

"Give his people the best treatment and tell my team to allow him to come up here. I wanna meet with this nigga personally just as bad."

He flopped down in his chair and pulled open the bottom drawer of his desk. He took out the Mach .10, slamming the clip inside of it. He could already feel his heart beating faster.

T.J. EDWARDS

Chapter 10

Chris stood up as Heinous stepped through the door with a mug on his dark-skinned face. His eyes were blood shot red and his face bore two teardrops on the left side of his face right   underneath the eye there. He had long dread locks that fell down his back, past his waist. His fit was all Gucci, black with hints of green speckled across it. His neck was full of gold, sprayed with green and yellow diamonds. He had a big blunt in his hand that looked like a brown Twinkie, the end already on fire. He gave Chris a look that said he didn't think shit of him.

"Please come in, homie. Let's have a talk," Chris said, thinking in his mind that he already didn't like the Jamaican.

He pushed the comfortable black seat away from his desk for the man could sit. Heinous then grabbed the chair roughly, mugging him for a minute. He then sat down before taking a strong pull from the weed stuffed cigar.

"So, you're the one they call Chris. Am I right?"

Chris's eyes bugged out of his head. He expected the Jamaican to have a strong accent, yet he sounded like he had been in the states for a long time. He wanted to ask him about that, but decided against it. He didn't like the way the man was looking at him, so he decided to address that.

"Say, what's all that mugging about, homie? You got a problem with me or something?"

Heinous laughed. He thought it was so cute when a nigga wanted to act all tough just to match his swagger. He could see right through Chris. He could tell that he wasn't about that street life. He might have had balls, but not the kind that Heinous was accustomed to cutting off. He would never make it in the slums of Jamaica Heinous thought. He laughed again.

"Boy, ya trust me. If I had a problem wit' you in any way, you'd be on the news already. The mug is natural on my face. I don't change it for nobody. That includes you." He took the smoke and blew it in Chris's direction.

Chris mugged him and sat down in his seat, then placed the Mach .10 on his lap. "So, what you wanna talk to me about, homie?"

Heinous took another pull from his blunt. He could feel the smoke invading his lungs almost choking him. The high was lovely. It felt like he was floating on a cloud. He felt righteous, ready to set the American in his place.

"I want this club and me won't take no for an answer. You're in my way and I don't like it."

He dumped the ashes of his blunt on to Chris's office floor and mugged him. Chris slid the ashtray across his desk fast and it landed in Heinous' lap.

"That's where you dump yo' ashes, nigga." He mugged him with hatred. "And as far as my club goes, how does 'hell no' work for you since the regular 'no' you won't take?"

Heinous picked the ashtray up over his head and slung it down with all of his might. It bounced off of the floor, flying against the wall.

"That's why I don't like you Chicago niggas. You're too cocky. Ya think that you're the only ones that kill with no hesitation. That everybody must follow somebody else instead of being your own boss. I know what you're used to dealing with, but I ain't that nigga. Now, I'm telling you that I want this club and a few more of the things that you and King have. I don't like you niggas. Neither did my Uncle Garvey or my cousin Minaj."

Chris's eyes got as big as saucers. He spoke about the crazy Jamaican regime that he and King had went to war with a few years back. It was the same regime that had murdered King's sister and mother. They were relentless and the head of their army was Garvey. Minaj was Garvey's sister who was crazier than him. At the mention of their names, Chris placed his finger on the trigger of his weapon, ready to pull it and splatter the Jamaican.

Heinous saw the look on his face and smiled. "That's right. So you know what my bloodline looks like."

Chris wiped the sweat off of his forehead. He wasn't afraid of Heinous, but now he knew for sure the man was well connected. To enter into a war with him would mean they would be   entering into a war with damn near the entire country of Jamaica.

He refused to show any signs of weakness in front of the man. He felt like panicking. He needed to get King on the phone as soon as possible. He knew he would know what to do. He couldn't wait to see how he would respond to who Heinous was and his relation to their former enemies. "Look, nigga. Like I said, you ain't taking my club and you ain't taking shit else from me or my nigga."

Heinous slammed his hand on top of Chris's desk so hard, the laptop fell off of it. He mugged him for a long time. "Are you sure about that?"

***

As soon as Greed finished telling her the news, Jersey fainted. He caught her and laid her on the bed. For the last hour, he held a cool towel against her forehead. Finally she eyes opened. "Greed? Greed?"

Greed took the towel away and looked down on her. "I'm right here, baby. I'm sitting right by your side. Talk to me."

She sat up in the bed of the motel room. "Baby, tell me it was just a dream. Tell me that our son is still alive, that some nigga ain't killed my baby." She looked hysterical like she was about to lose her mind.

Greed rubbed her face with his thumbs. Wiping her tears away, he shook his head no. "He's gone, baby."

Jersey shot out of the bed and fell to her knees, sobbing loudly. "Noooooo! Noooooo! Not my baby. He's just a little, bitty, baby boy. He's mine. I gave birth to him. Nobody should be able to take him away from me. It's not fair. He's my child. I miss him so bad!" She rocked back and forth, crying her eyes out.

Greed lowered himself down to his knees with tears rolling down his cheeks. His heart was heavy. He had lost his baby boy, the kid that reminded him so much of himself. It was tearing him apart. It seemed like it was hard for him to imagine him as a grown man. He kept on see Ajani as a baby or a toddler, trying to learn how to walk. That was his heart. He crawled over to Jersey and pulled her into his embrace while her body shook against him in obvious pain.

"Whhyyyyy? Whhyyyyy my baby? Why my child? Oh, I love him so much, Greed. He's our little man. Ohhhh! Lord, it hurts so bad! I can't take this shit!" She tried to get up, but he held her tighter.

"Baby, I know you're in pain. We're both hurting, but it's going to be alright. Somebody is going to pay for these sins against us. Somebody gone pay for hurting our family," Greed told her, feeling the snot run out of his nose. It dripped down to his top lip before he sniffed it back up into his nostrils.

Jersey shook her head, squeezing her eyelids together. "No. No. I can't take this shit. I never thought it would hurt this much. I gave birth to that boy. I held him inside of my body for nearly ten months. I almost died trying to push him out. He's my little man. I nursed him, I gave him my all and now they took him away." She tried fighting Greed to break away free from his hold. "Get off of me, Greed! Get off of me! I'm finna go find the nigga that did this myself!"

Greed held her tighter and cried, holding his wife. The pain was extremely intense.

* * *

"Averie, I'm about to tell you something, baby and I don't want you to freak out. I need for you to be strong and to know that everything is going to be okay once we get through this," Rayjon said, trying his best to keep his composure intact. He felt himself losing the battle.

Averie sat up on the bed and ran her hands over

her face. She had hoped Rayjon would stop through and give her a little dick. Now, he was making it seem like he was about to give her some kind of news that would break her down. She tried her best to brace herself, but just reading his face was scaring the living daylights out of her. "Tell me what's going on, baby. I'm scared."

Rayjon tried to walk to her side the best he could, but his knees got weak, causing him to fall to the floor on them. "They kilt Ajani. They kilt my brother, man. My Pops said they just found him and both of my Aunties dead. I don't know what to do." He squeezed his eyelids together and tried to breathe, but it was a heavy task.

Averie's eyes were bucked. It took her a moment to process what was going on and then she felt sick. Her entire relationship with Ajani played over and over in her mind, the good times and the bad. Then she thought about him being murdered and as crazy as it seemed, she felt no emotions at all. She felt she was all cried out over her son, leaving none for him.

Rayjon rocked back and forth, missing his brother. He felt deeply wounded, wishing he could hug him one more time. He wished that he could tell him that he loved him one more time, but he couldn't. He didn't know how he would go forward in life without his right hand.

Averie rubbed his back. She wanted to do as much as she could to comfort him. She hated to see him break down the way he did. She wished she could take the pain for him, but that was not possible. For her, she was over Ajani. He had taken her through so much, that his even death barely grazed her. She felt some sense of joy that he was out of the picture, allowing Rayjon to be all hers. She didn't want to share him with anybody. She wanted him all to herself and felt like that would be the only way he would stay alive. The longer he ran behind his family, the closer he would come to death. It was time to remove himself from the game.

Rayjon sat up and smiled, tears running down his cheeks. "We gotta kill this nigga, man. Whoever did this to my brother don't know who they fucking with. We'll never take this shit   lying down! Never!"

Averie wrapped him into her arms. He sobbed into her neck as she rubbed his back. She knew that he was hurting. And as mad as he was, she also knew he was worried. Worried   because he didn't really know who had hit his brother or what they were up against. He kept on saying things like "whoever did this", and "they don't know who they're fucking with". Had he known any of it, he would have put a name to whoever did it already. "Baby, can you listen to me for a minute?"

Rayjon took his head back and looked her in the eyes. His chest continued to heave up and down. "What's good, man?"

She looked over his face with deep concern. She felt the strong love a woman felt for a man who had taken over her heart.

"Baby, I want you to listen to me." She rubbed his face with her soft thumbs. Rayjon gave her a look that told her to go on. He kept on having flashes of his brother running through his memory. He missed him so bad. He wished they'd never had that fight.

All he wanted to do was hug him in that moment and kiss him all over his cheeks the way he used to when they were little.

"Baby, do you remember what you were saying about sending me down to Miami, so I could get away from all of this bull crap?"

Rayjon nodded. "Yeah, I do. What about it?"

"Well, I think that me and you should bounce tonight. Let's just get on a plane and leave this city behind. This ain't where it's at no more. We have to be smart. Let's do it together, please."

Rayjon tried to snatch away from her, but she held his arm. "Baby, just listen to me. There are already too many that have been killed. Do you wanna be next? Huh? Do you wanna leave me like that?" She felt the tears sailing down her face, making it hard for her to see.

Rayjon yanked away and stood up. "You expect to me to just roll over and let this fuck nigga kill my brother, my heart? Me and my brother been through it all together. I always been there for him and he always is there for me. Now, when he needs me the most I'm just supposed to go to some beach and lay back in the in the sun while he is resting in peace? Fuck that!"

Averie saw him reaching towards the bed to grab his jacket, so she grabbed his arm. "So, that mean its fuck me then.?" She stood in his face. "All my life I been afraid to stand up to any man that could hurt me, fearing that I wasn't strong enough to do it. Well, I'm tired of being this weak female. I'm taking my stand with you. If you wanna get out of this house, you gone have to kill me because I ain't letting you. You told me that you loved me. You told me that you would   always protect me and my heart. Well, if I allow you to walk out of that door, you're going to do both."

Rayjon lowered his head as more tears fell from his eyes.

"Averie, move out of my face and let me go handle my business. I gotta stand beside my family. It's my job."

Averie turned around and reached under the bed, putting the .380 pistol into her hand then handing it to him. "Here, if you wanna go out that door, all I ask is that you blow my brains out because if you won't, when you leave out, I will." She was ready to go. She had a feeling in the pit of her stomach that if Rayjon left out of that door, that he wasn't coming back ever again. She felt like she couldn't live without him. She refused, too.

Rayjon felt himself on the verge of breaking down. After losing his brother, he knew he needed Averie and that losing her would have been way too much for him. She was the only person keeping him strong. He could have turned to his mother, but she already had his father, Greed.

"You said you love me, Rayjon. Well, I love you too, baby and I need you. I need you to leave with me. I need for us to get on as soon as possible and get the fuck out of here. Please, I am begging you on my knees."

She dropped down and grabbed his hand that was holding the gun. "Or if you won't, please put me out of my misery right now. Just grant me that one wish, then you can go and be with your family because I belong to you, not to them."

Rayjon stood there for a long time, holding the gun. He didn't know what to do. On one hand, be didn't want to turn his back on his family. He felt he had to be there for them at all costs, especially since they were under attack. That was the time when families were supposed to pull together even stronger. It wasn't the time for one of them to flee like a coward off into the sunset with a female. It just didn't look right.

But at the same time, he was tired of it all. All of the killing, all of the running, all of the hiding and switching states. He just wanted to be free of it all. He wanted to sit back and live a normal life, one where he could love normally and be loved normally. Not a life where his love was based on blood and carnage.

He looked down at Averie and saw the tears in her eyes. Her beautiful face was full of pain and worry. She really did love him like no other. He could tell that. She needed him just as much as he needed her. He also knew she was meant to be his wife somewhere down the road if Jehovah allowed him to live that long.

She picked up his hand and made him put the barrel of the gun to her forehead. "Kill me, baby because I can't stand for you to break my heart or we leave this city and this life behind. What are you gonna do?"

* * *

Aiden could hear the loud music resonating down

the alley. He crept down, trying his best to stay low against the wall. Greed had given him the order to assassinate Yayo. He had tracked the man, finding him at the studio only ten minutes prior. He watched him enter into the studio through what appeared to a back entrance. He had a crew of about five men. Three of them were big enough to be football players.

Aiden guessed they had to be some sort of security for him. Either way, he didn't care. Just like the rest of the family, he was experiencing a heavy heart because of what happened to Ajani. The only thing on his mind was murder.

Greed knew he didn't have to tag along with Aiden whenever he sent him on a mission   because the young man was deadly. In fact, he moved better alone. That's the way it had always been. Aiden waited until about three of the men went into the studio, leaving two outside to guard the door. He then slid the sharp scalpel out of his sleeve and lowered his eyes.

T.J. EDWARDS

Chapter 11

He knelt down and got as close to them as possible before he stood up, nearly causing them to jump out of their skin. One of the men who looked to be every bit of seven feet tall closed
the door and looked down at him with anger. He had to be every bit of three hundred plus pounds. He had on an all-black shirt that read "Security" on it.

"May I help you, lil' nigga?" he asked, looking like an angry gorilla.

Aiden looked up to him and lowered his eyes, slitting them. "Say, that's Yayo in there right?" He just wanted to confirm his mark although he had matched the man's face to the pictures Greed had sent him on his phone already.

Monster mugged him with irritation. "We ain't got time for no groupies, nigga. It's two in the morning and cold. You gotta get the fuck out of our alley. Yayo ain't got no time for niggas like you tonight." He pushed Aiden slightly in the chest. "Get yo' ass out of here lil' yellow nigga. Word is bond. "

Low stepped up. "Yeah, keep it moving lil' nigga before we have to whoop yo' ass out here." He shook his head. "These gay mafuckas be killing me. Here this nigga is out two in the morning trying to see Yayo. That shit is gay as hell. I should whoop-you on the strength," Low said, mugging Aiden with hatred.

He stepped towards him, ready to smack the living daylights out of him. While they respected Yayo with all that they were, they hated he had chosen to purchase a studio in an area where the gay community was heavy. They could never tell what was what or who was who. They simply guessed that since Aiden was out in the middle of the night asking to see Yayo, he had to be sweet on some level.

Aiden stood there with his head down just listening to them speak. He hated bullies of all kinds. He had been bullied ever since he could remember. They talked about him because he was lighter than everybody else. They made fun of his acne. They made fun of him having a white father. They picked on his brother and every day the kids found a way to make school a living hell until he started killing them.

Monster stepped forward ready to choke Aiden to get his point across. "Like I said, lil' nigga. Get the fuck out this—Ack! Arrrrgh! Ooh! Uh!"

Aiden grabbed the side of his face, taking the scalpel and slicing his throat from one end all the way to the other. He went back again before pushing him in the chest and stabbing him in his left eye.

It popped out immediately as he yanked the scalpel back out. He sliced his throat four quick times, watching him fall to the ground. As he held his neck, the blood spurted through his fingers and dripped off of his wrist.

Monster saw the man reach out to touch him, feeling his hand on his face as the blade cut   into his throat. He wanted to holler and tell him to tell him to back up, but he felt the pain. It felt like he had the worst sore throat of his life.

Then the hot fluid spilled into his windpipe, choking him. Before he could adjust to the feeling, the blade came back again and again, opening him up. He saw himself falling, the concrete coming fast. Then his face went crashing into it while his blood spurted up like a sprinkler. His last thoughts were of his new-born daughter before he faded to black.

Low saw the yellow man slice his homie's throat. He felt it was his business to jump in there and help him, but he was too quick. He saw the point of the blade corning at him fast. It landed in his eye and he heard it pop loudly, almost like a firecracker in his brain. The pain shot to the back of his brain, then all around. Before he could scream, he felt the blade slicing him open four quick times. His head fell backwards while he dropped to his knees, holding his throat. The hot blood coursed through his fingers and saturated his coat. He fell forward and landed on his cheek. He could still hear the music from the studio. He started singing along with the song   before he faded away.

Aiden dragged Low by his legs until he was away from the door. Then he picked him up and dumped him into the big metal garbage can before going back and doing the same to Monster. He closed the lid and made his way to the studio door, opening it up just to take a peek. He saw another big man sitting at desk looking at his phone. He appeared to be the only one in the room. Beside him was a water cooler and a big screen television that was showing Sports Center.

Aiden took the .45 from the small of his back and twisted on the silencer. He figured since he'd already killed two men, the one sitting at the desk would be the third. Then there would   only be two more left guarding Yayo. He couldn't wait to get to all of them. He had visions of one of them harming his deceased mother, making him curl his upper lip in hatred.

Wayne hated getting into a text war with his

wifey. She seemed to catch an attitude every time he had to work late at the studio with Yayo. He figured she thought he was out cheating, so in order to ease her mind, he decided that he would sit and text to her as much as possible. That way she would know that he wasn't on no dumb shit.

He was reading her last response when all of the sudden it felt like he had been stabbed in the forehead by a screw driver. His head yanked backwards and heard a loud screaming bell. He felt dizzy, wanting to throw up. Everything turned red. Then he saw his cheek fly off as he was fell backwards. He looked up in time to see a yellow angry face looking down on him before there was fire and he faded to black.

Aiden had closed one eye, aiming and firing. The first bullet slammed into Wayne's forehead causing blood to shoot out the back of his head and onto the wall behind his desk, yet the man didn't fall.

Aiden was impressed and pissed off at the same time. He aimed again and shot, the bullets connecting and ripping half of his face off. Finally, Wayne fell backwards. Aiden jogged over to his fallen body and popped him three more times before ducking down.

Paper walked into the lobby of the studio with a bad feeling in his gut. He figured he would check on his other homies just to make sure that everything was good. But as soon as he got into the lobby where Wayne worked, he smelled the blood.

It smelled like a bunch of pennies were on fire mixed with sweat and mucous. He walked further into the lobby and saw Wayne slumped behind the desk with half of his head blown off. He looked like he had swallowed dynamite.

"Holy shit!" He turned to go and alert the others, but felt an arm wrap around his neck, then what felt like a hundred stabs on his temple. The first one punctured his brain, causing blood to pour out of his ear. Then there was blood coming out of his eyes and more stabbing. He tried to holler for help, but his throat was cut. After falling backwards, he felt a heavy weight on his chest, then pokes all over his face.

Aiden sized up the fat man immediately. As soon as he turned on the balls of his feet to go get help, Aiden shot up and wrapped his arm around his neck, taking the scalpel and jamming it into his temple. The soft tissue gave way easily. Then he was stabbed again and again, hitting all brain and bone before slicing his throat and slinging him to the ground. He had visions of his mother, then visions of Ajani, causing him to hate the men even more.

He stepped on the man's chest and took the .45 back out of the small of his back. He unscrewed the silencer. He wanted to hear some noise. There was only one other man besides Yayo. He never did like silencers. He felt like they took the fun out of the murder. Noise is what made it feel real to him. He needed to hear it. Needed to feel his murders. He was obsessed with it.

He knelt down and crept to the door of the studio. He twisted the knob and to his surprise, it opened right up. There was an engineer working the controls in one room with Yayo on the other side of the glass rapping his heart out. Aiden smiled for a brief second before turning it into a sadistic frown. He slipped all the way into the room with the engineer and slowly walked over to him.

Swiss was nodding his head to the music. He felt that Yayo finally was getting into the groove of things. He was vibing with him. Quiet as it was kept, he felt like it was a lost cause. He knew that his career wasn't going anywhere. The nigga was washed up. No matter how many of his hot beats he put behind him, it didn't do any good. The world had moved on to that Migos kind of rap. It was fucked up, but it was what it was.

Swiss felt something sharp stab him in the shoulder, then he was being picked up in the air like a rag doll being thrown face first into the glass of the booth. His head was yanked backward by his hair then he felt the blade slicing him from one ear all the way to the other. He started throwing up plasma. Stomping his feet holding his neck, he got dizzier and dizzier until he fell to his knees missing his wife and his children. His heart started to beat really fast, then all at once it stopped and so did his thinking.

Yayo stood looking out at Swiss as the big yellow man came into the room. When he reached him, he watched him slammed a knife into his shoulder. Then picked him up effortlessly and threw him into the glass on the other side, before smiling at him and cutting into his throat. His blood sprayed the glass. It dripped down as if it were red window cleaner. Swiss took a step back, holding his throat. Blood poured out from him as he seemed to dance before falling to the floor.

Yayo had been watching all of his antics so much so, that he'd lost track of the yellow man. He looked around in a panic with his high completely blown. When he turned around and saw Aiden looking down at him, he pissed on himself.

Aiden grabbed him by the throat and held him in the air with one hand while his feet dangled in the air. "You had something to do with my family being attacked. You must pay." He squeezed his throat harder and harder.

Yayo could feel the bones in his neck cracking. He started to panic. He wiggled his legs and hit at Aiden's hands to no avail. No matter what he did, the man would not drop him until he hoisted him up and threw him all the way across the room and into the glass.

Yayo flew into the glass, feeling the wind fly out of him. His back slammed into it hard. He rolled until he was on his side, struggling to get up. "Yo, what's your problem, kid? What beef you got wit me?"

Aiden slowly walked over to him, watching Yayo struggle to get up. As soon as he did, he threw his guards up and made it seem like he wanted to fight. Aiden smiled at this. It had been a long time since he had ripped a man apart.

Yayo threw up his guards and ran towards Aiden swinging wildly. His first punch caught the man in the jaw. His second caught him in the eye. He jumped back to see what damage was done. Aiden winced, and 'nodded his head. He had not even taken a step back. In his mind, Yayo hit like a bitch and he needed to step his game up.

He waited until Yayo gathered himself. Then he walked back toward him. If Yayo wasn't afraid before, now he was spooked. He felt like he needed to get the fuck out of there. He was hysterical, in a frenzy with panic. He ran up on Aiden and swung, then wished he never had. Aiden caught his fist and crushed it in the palm of his hand. He could feel his bones popping and crunching together. Yayo screamed out like a bitch. It was hilarious.

He then felt himself being picked up into the air, then brought down at full speed onto the top of his head. All he saw was the studio from an upside down angle before the ground came fast and bussed his head wide open. He felt extremely woozy.

The yellow man straddled him, putting eight fingers into his mouth. Next, he started to pull upward and downward with some much strength, he heard his jaws popping and cracking loudly.

The pain started almost immediately. It hurt so bad that he was in tears. He had no idea why it was happening to him. There was more crunching and popping as the bone on the left side of his face broke away from his skull loudly, yet Aiden kept on pulling.

The bottom part of his mouth popped and broke away from the top of his jaw. Aiden put his knee in his mouth and kept on pulling it apart. There was cracking, crunching and loud popping as his bones broke away from one another, shattering his jaw and the lower parts of his skull.

"Arrrrrghhhh!"

Crack, crack, crack.

"Argghh!"

Aiden ripped his mouth completely apart, stood up and stuck his entire shoe down his throat while Yayo's body hopped up and down as blood covered the room. Aiden looked down on him with his chest heaving up and down. All he could think about was becoming head of the Ski Mask Cartel. He felt he was more than ready.

* * *

Greed handed Jersey the bowl of soup, and rubbed her back. "How are you feeling this morning, baby?"

She turned away from him after shrugging her shoulders. "I don't know. I'm still really sick and I don't feel like eating, so don't try and make me," she said, feeling like she was getting ready to puke.

Greed frowned. "Baby, you know you got low iron just like me. You gotta eat something or you gone keep on passing out. Now, you know I can't allow that, so let's go." He pulled her by the shoulder and she jerked away from him.

"Greed, I'm not eating that shit and if you try and make me, I'm gone throw up everywhere. I'm not kidding." She put a pillow over her head.

Greed took it off and threw it across the room. "You finna eat something. I know what my woman needs in order to stay healthy and it's my job to make sure that you get it. Now, get yo' ass over here and eat this soup."

She turned over and sat up. "Fine, but if I throw up, it's on you."

Greed spooned the soup and put it to her mouth for her to eat. At first she didn't want to open it, but slowly her lips parted and he slid the spoon inside of it.

"Here, now swallow and try your best to not throw it back up. It ain't no way we gone be able to master this situation if we're weak. Now, I need you stronger than what you are."

Jersey blinked tears. She was missing Ajani so bad that she didn't know what to do. Then Greed was talking about them not having a funeral. He figured they would just bury him in a grave somewhere. She hated the idea. She felt the soup on her tongue and gagged.

"I don't want that shit and why aren't we burying my son the right way? Why are we treating him like some animal unworthy of a proper burial? White folks do more for their pets than what we're doing for our own child and that's bothering me." She pushed the bowl of soup out of her face and stood up, pacing along the side of the bed, tears already pouring down her cheeks. "This shit ain't sitting right with me. Why are we in this room and our son's killer is out there probably laid up with a bunch of bitches, celebrating the fact that he got over on our family?"

Greed took a deep breath, trying to calm his temper. Jersey was trying his patience. He loved his wife with all that was in him. But there were times when she really got the best of him, making it hard for him to not snap out on her. He reminded himself she was still going through the grieving process and that he needed to be as understanding as much as he could.

"Baby, how about you chill?" He said this without even looking up at her. The soup had spilled all over the bed and he felt himself getting hot.

Jersey stopped mid-way, placing her hand on her

hip.

"That's the best you got Greed, huh? You want me to chill?" She sucked her teeth. "Maybe that's the problem. We around this mafucka chilling too much. So much so, niggas are actually killing us off. My sister, now my son. Who's next? Me? You? Rayjon?"

At saying his name, she almost threw up. She imagined something happening to him and nearly lost her mind. She got scared and her heart started to beat so fast in her chest, that it hurt.

Greed took a deep breath and slowly blew it out. He had so many things going through his mind that he had a hard time focusing on one at a time. The more she talked, the angrier he   became until he felt he was seconds away from snatching her up and putting her in her place.

"You ain't the same man I remember. You used to be a straight goon, fucking niggas over on a daily basis. I have washed so many niggas' blood out of your clothes. Now other niggas' bitches are washing our family's blood out of theirs. This shit sucks. I never thought I would see the day when that would happen.

Chapter 12

Greed snatched her up so fast, she couldn't even finish her sentence. He sat on the bed pulling her over his lap before pulling her nightgown up, baring her naked brown ass cheeks. He wrapped his leg around her ankle, raised his hand and brought it down hard on to her skin. It sounded like someone had clapped their hands together real loud. Jersey felt the stinging pain on her rear end and shrieked out loud, throwing her head back. Before she could get used to the pain, he whacked her again and again and again.

"I. Don't. Know. Who. The. Fuck. You. Think. You. Talking. To. Like. That. But. I'm. Still. Yo'. Muthafucking. Daddy. And. I. Run. This. Shit!"

Whack. Whack. Whack. Whack.

The hard slaps he gave made her ass jiggle, then turn a reddish brown. The pain was unbearable, enough to make her close her eyes and cry real tears. "Please, Greed! I'm sorry, Daddy! I'm sorry! Please don't do me like this," ,she whimpered.

Her cries fell on deaf ears. Greed continued to attack that ass for a full five minutes. By that time, Jersey's was having a fit, sobbing like a big baby. He stopped his assault and rubbed all over her thick ass cheeks while she cried under him. They felt hot on his palm. He squeezed them, then felt in between her middle. Her pussy was so wet that as soon as he touched it, the juices stuck to his fingers and dripped off of his wrist.

He took two of them and massed them around in her gap, taking his leg from around her   ankles. Her clit stood erect and angry. He pinched it and rubbed his thumb over it a few times.

"Ummm, Daddy. Why you always gotta do me like this? Don't you know that your baby girl is hurting?" She opened her legs and arched her back. She could feel her juices dripping down her thighs. She was almost embarrassed. This was a time for grieving, yet there she was so aroused that she wished he had stuck four fingers into her small hole.

Greed slapped that ass before spreading her cheeks apart. He played over her pussy lips, trapping them between his thumb and forefinger, pulling them a little bit before squeezing them together, causing her juices leaked out of her. "I think you just need some of Daddy, baby. I think you just need me to knock this box out so I can remind you who the fuck I am. Is that it?" His dick was so hard that it was hurting him.

Jersey felt him slide two fingers into her hole. She moaned so loud, she shocked herself. It felt so good. She wanted him to ram them in there, to hurt her a little bit, taking away some of her mental pain. She needed him to punish her. "Daddy, Daddy. I need you to stop playing with me. I need you to get up here and hurt me from the back. Fuck away my pain. Make me feel like a little protected girl. Help me believe that my Daddy got me and that we're safe from here on out. I need you so bad," she whimpered.

Greed had already slipped down his Robert Cavalli jeans and kicked his boxers to the side. His dick stood all the way up past his navel. The head was breathing, looking like an angry monster. He stroked it up and down and watched her brown lips part from the back, revealing her wet pink essence. He was about to fuck her harder than he had ever fucked her before. He needed her just as bad as she needed him.

Jersey felt his fat head on her opening. She reached back and pulled her ass apart, revealing her fat pussy she knew had always drove him crazy. She felt his dick slowly entering into her.

"Daddy, stop playing with me and beat this pussy up! Come on now! I need you and only you can make me feel the way! I need to! Now, come on!" She screamed and moaned, reaching underneath herself to play with her fat clit.

Greed sucked his middle finger, pulled it out of his mouth and slid it into her ass before cocking his hips back, slamming forward so hard that she screamed. "Yes! Fuck yes! Oh my God, Daddy!" She felt him grip her hips, then he went crazy inside the pussy.

Bam! Bam! Bam! Bam! Bam! Bam! Bam! Bam!

He went again and again with no mercy. She pinched her own clit while he smacked her ass, and grabbed her hair roughly.

"Awww! Awww! Shit, Daddy! Yes! Please fuck yo' baby girl! This that shit I'm talking about right here! Yes!" She slammed back into him to meet his huge dick as it bored into her body. Tear rain out of her eyes, and the feeling in her pussy told her that he was doing his job.

Greed felt her walls tightening around him. Her juices ran out of her, making it slippery, but he still grabbed them hips and got to fucking her so hard, veins appeared in his neck. That pussy was good and hot, the smell coming from her sex was enough to drive him crazy. He loved her natural scent. He smacked her on the ass again and again, spanking her because he knew that's what kept that pussy wet. "I'm Daddy! Tell me who I am, baby girl. Tell Daddy right now!"

Jersey was fingering her clit hard. Her vagina's nipple was standing up like a little penis. It vibrated, and the throbbing inside of it was driving her crazy. Then the smacks on her ass was adding to it all. His big dick was opening her up wide, touching regions in her that only he could reach. She felt full. She felt used. And on top of that, she felt loved and treated all at the same time. He was fucking her like a gangsta, murdering that pussy. She felt him yank her head backwards by grabbing a handful of her hair. That made her scream again before coming hard on his dick.

Bam! Bam! Bam!

"Tell me I'm Daddy! I ain't gone tell you no more!"

His abs were popping. His huge biceps tensed up. He looked like a body builder with dimples. Sweat poured down his massive chest and along his back. He continued to lunge forward, making sure that his dick was hitting her deepest spots. He loved his wife. There was no doubt about that. He would kill a mafucka for or about her any day of the week and had already done so many times before. The fact that she was starting to doubt his ability to protect the family was messing with his head and then some. He sped up the pace and really started to murder her.

"You're my daddy! On my God! Sheeitttt!

Awww! I'm coming again, Daddddeee!" She screamed as her breasts started to come out of her gown. Her body was being rocked, yet she continued to play with her clit. It was the best feeling in the world, one that Greed had taught her to do and enjoy.

"I'm coming, baby girl! Daddy coming! Here I come, baby! Fuck, here I come!" He sped up the pace.

Bam! Bam! Bam! Bam!

He slapped her one more time on the ass and slid two fingers deep into her back door before coming so hard that his abs locked up. His chest muscles jumped again and again. He fell on top of her, his dick deep in her belly.

* * *

Ding-dong!

Big Momma turned the fire down on the stove and wiped her hands on her apron. She looked at her watch and noted that it was only four o'clock in the afternoon. She wouldn't have dinner ready for another hour. She wondered who it was at the door.

Percy slowly came down the steps after taking a nice dump in the bathroom. It was Sunday and he had to make room for his wife's Sunday dinner. There wasn't nothing like it and hadn't been for the last thirty years. He could smell the aroma of the glazed ham in the air along with the cornbread. He licked his lips and figured he'd put his dentures in at another time.

Big Momma went to the door and look out of the window after pulling the yellow curtain back. She looked into the face of a handsome man that resembled Idris Alba. He smiled at her and adjusted his tie. He looked like one of the deacons at the church. They had just got a bunch of new male members that had come over from Trenton, a bunch of fine young upstanding men or so she was told. Before she could even go against her better judgment, she opened the door.

King couldn't believe his luck. As soon as he heard the front door opening, he got excited. He tightened his gloves on his hand, preparing himself. He already had the location of where Greed and his wife were staying, but before he finished them off, he wanted to add insult to injury. Killing his grandmother would be a delicious victory for King. No man could think straight while they were angry. It was nearly impossible to strategize.

Percy made his way down the steps and had to take a breather. Pretty soon he wanted them to consider getting the contraption that stuck to the banister so they could sit down on it, taking them up and down the stairs. He wiped the sweat from his forehead.

"Girl, who is that at the door? You opening it all willy nilly. I hope it ain't no more of them church folk. Coming over here eating up all the food that Jehovah blessed us with. Now, I'm all about the brethren, but when it comes to eating up my food, I'm about ready to find another church home. I'm telling you."

He took a seat in the small sofa before his eyes got as big as saucers. He watched a man step into the house and grab his wife by the throat, picking her all the way up into the air, holding her there. She kicked at him and tried to scream, but her teeth fell out of her mouth, bouncing off of his forehead. That must of made the man angry because in one toss, he threw her into the big screen T.V. in the living room with a loud crash. It exploded right away and blew her backwards.

Percy tried to get up, but his back locked up on him, making it difficult for him to move.

"You son of a bitch. You leave my Sugah alone. She ain't did nothing to you. Now, gone get!" He tried once again to get out of the chair and made it to a half stance before his legs gave out.

King mugged the man as he rubbed his forehead. He looked him over closely, figuring he wouldn't be a problem because he could barely move. He smiled at that and turned his sights on the old woman who was struggling like hell to get to her feet. The burnt smell of the television was all through the house. It was giving him a headache.

He waited until she was on all four before he walked over and pulled her up by the hair. "So you're Greed's mother, huh?"

She winced in pain. "That's my grandbaby. His mother passed away a long time ago. And his name ain't no damn Greed. His name is Thelonious. I hate when you thugs call him that."

King looked her over in admiration. He had to honor the fact that she was so tough, even for an old woman. It made him smile. She tried to jerk away from him. "Let me go, young man. What business do you have with me?"

"My business isn't with just you per se, but your

blood line. You are simply caught in the middle of something bigger than you," King said, getting a better grip. He looked over at the old man. He was still trying to come to a stand.

Big Momma yanked her head back, only to have him tighten his grip. "You ain't bigger than Jesus." She smacked at his hand. "You ain't nothing but a weapon of the devil and my God told me that no weapons formed against me shall prosper." She cocked back and kicked him so hard in the nuts, that he released her and fell on his face, squirming around the floor in pain. He even threw up a little.

Big Momma ran in the kitchen and grabbed her biggest pot, one that she used to cook her turkeys in. She stood over King, raised it and brought it down over his head.

Whoom!

The hit rattled King's brain. He was still shaken up from the kick to the nuts, so when the pan hit him, it damn near knocked the understanding out of his head.

"No weapon formed against me shall prosper!" She brought the pot down again, this time splitting his head wide open. Blood poured down his neck. He got dizzy and the room turned upside down. "No weapons formed against me shall prosper. I rebuke you Satan in the Mighty name of Jesus!" She brought the pot down so hard, it knocked him out cold.

* * *

"Hello. Hello. Grandma? Where y'all at?" Dawn asked, taking off her coat and putting it on the rack.

She picked her baked macaroni and cheese dish up off the floor and made her way into the kitchen. when she saw King come up to a sitting position, he took his hand and patted his forehead, covering it in blood.

"Oh my God! What happened to you?" she said, setting the dish on the table and running to his side into a squatting position.

To King, it looked like there were three of her. He felt incredibly woozy, the world spinning around him. "Somebody attacked me. I can't see. Blood running in my eyes."

Dawn helped him to stand up. "Come on. Let's get you to the couch." Once he was up, she helped him to walk as he leaned on her for support. To her, he felt like he was packed with muscle. Dawn couldn't understand how anybody could have managed to attack him and live to tell the story.

King allowed her to help him get to the couch before he laid back his head. She sat him on the same couch the old man had been sitting on. Then it him all at once. *The old people? Where had they gone? And how long had he been out*? he started asking to himself as he began to panic. He tried to get up, but a wave of dizziness came over him before he fell back into the chair.

Dawn forced him to sit down. "Hey, just chill, man. I'm about to call the police and ambulance. They should be here any minute. You just gotta hold on."

King wiped the blood out of his face. "No! You can't do that!" he said, getting up and fighting through the dizziness.

Now Dawn was starting to panic. "Wait a minute.

Why not?"

All of the sudden, she was starting to fear for her safety, wondering where were her   grandparents, if they were they okay, and why would a suspicious man was laid out on their floor with blood running out of his head. None of it added up the right way.

"Dawn, no! That man tried to kill us!" Big Momma said, corning up from the basement. She had just finished calling the police and they were on their way. She'd heard her   granddaughter-in-law's voice through the vents. She knew she had to get up there to save her before the crazy man fully recovered.

Dawn felt like she was going to shit on herself. She made a move to run to her grandmother when she felt King grab her by the microbraids, pulling her back to him. He wrapped his huge bicep around her neck and squeezed. The bones in her neck started to crack and pop.

"Ackk! Ackk! I can't breathe," she gasped, smacking at his huge arm.

Big Momma ran into the kitchen and grabbed a knife. She wasn't like Percy. She was eight years younger and a whole lot more mobile. She had her mind set on cutting the man up. She'd watched her late husband do it many of times, back in the old days before she was saved and filled with the Holy Ghost.

King squeezed Dawn's throat so hard that it snapped. He wrapped his arm under her chin and pulled it backwards with all of his might before twisting it all the way to the right. A bone popped out of the skin in her neck. She fell to the floor with her eyes wide open, drool pouring out of mouth.

Dawn had beat and beat at his arm as her air-waves began to block. She couldn't breathe. She couldn't stop herself from panicking. Then she heard the bones popping in her neck and her spine locked up. There was a loud ringing in her ears, her toes going numb. The man squeezed harder and harder. She couldn't think. She felt her brain expanding, then the vessels in her eyes popped and everything turned blue. Her neck popped again, then she felt him forcing her head all the way to the right until her chin was behind her back. Her bone broke off, sticking out through the skin in her neck. Her last sights were of her grandmother-in-law running into the room with a butcher's knife.

King threw Dawn to the floor hard and mugged the old woman who had a menacing scowl on her face. "You want some of this, old lady? Come on, let's get it in." Blood dripped into his eye and he could barely stand up straight.

Big Momma slowly walked up to him and took a deep breath. "Come on, Satan! I ain't scared of you. This house belongs to Jesus, so you can leave us be!"

She lashed and sliced him on the arm. King jumped back and watched his blood come through the slit. He looked at the old woman in amazement. He couldn't believe she had enough gall to do such a thing. Before he could gather himself, she sliced him again, this time on the shoulder. The blade was so sharp, it was like she had been sharpening it all day long.

"Get thee behind me, Satan. Get thee behind me right now! My house belongs to Jesus and forever will."

She lunged at him and King jumped back outta reach, stepping forward and punching her so hard that she flew backward, spitting her teeth into the air. She flipped over the table and landed on her back hard. King curled his upper lip before falling on his ass. The room was spinning worse than ever. Big Momma struggled to get up, her back locking up twice. She smacked her gums together and ran her tongue over him. "You done made me spit out my teeth. "

King came over and grabbed her by her thick, nappy, gray afro, pulling her up. He picked her up into the air and power bombed her on her neck through the glass table.   Glass shot everywhere. He fell on his ass, and got back up. "Uh. Uh. Uh."

Blood dripped into his eyes. He could hear the sounds of police sirens in the distance. He knew they had to be close. He picked her up again, watching the glass fall off of her body. He hoisted her into the air before bringing her down at full speed right on the top of her head.

The impact caused her head to smash into her shoulders, forcing her spine cord to snap as it broke away from her back. Before her feet even hit the floor, she was dead. King rushed and carved Greed's name in both, Big Momma and Dawn's forehead, before hitting it out the back door.

Chapter 13

Caspur was super wasted. He could barely stand up on his own two feet. Luckily, he had two of the baddest strippers in New York to hold him up. "Say, mane. Y'all help me get the fuck in this Limo, then I wanna see y'all fuck each other. Bring a little Tennessee to the Big Apple."

Trixie licked her lips, and kissed him on the cheek. "Whatever you want, baby. It's yo' world."

Cookie mugged her and gave her a look that said she didn't know if she was with all of that. It was only her fourth week at the club and females still weren't attractive to her. She just needed to pay off her rent for the month and if Caspur wasn't putting up them chips, then she wasn't fucking with him on that level. "Girl, how much he gone pay us to do all of that?" she asked loud enough for him to hear her.

Caspur turned up his double cup. "Mane, just know you straight. I still got a few chips tucked away. You hoez get down the way you supposed too and I'll give y'all a gee a piece. What dat sound like?"

Trixie reached and grabbed his dick. It sound like we about to put a show on for your money." As she said this, the stretched Navigator pulled up to the curb and the driver got out, opening the door for them.

Cookie found it odd that the driver had on regular street clothes with a pair of Vans. She was accustomed to seeing the drivers out in New York rocking high-end business suits, depending on the company. She shrugged her shoulders and took it to mean that

Caspur was just trying to keep it hood.

August closed the door behind them and walked around to the front of the limo before pulling away from the curb into the night with Times Square behind them. Caspur shook his head trying to get some of the sleepiness away from him. The Lean had his eyelids heavy. He could barely keep them open. It felt like the heat was turned all the way up. It was cooking him.

August turned the dial all the way to the max. He made sure the heat was back there cooking them. He saw the state of Caspur and knew the man was fucked up. The heat would only add to his high, or drunk feeling.

"Yo, fa real, B. It's super hot back here. What's good with yo' driver, Caspur?" Cookie asked, removing her Burberry jacket. She had sweat along her forehead and her titties felt like they were sweating too.

"Yeah, Caspur. Tell that nigga to turn this mafucking heat off. We about to die back here," Trixie said, getting on to her knees in front of Cookie.

She felt like the sooner she ate the bitch pussy, the faster everything would be over and done with. She didn't want to make a whole night out of it. She had to get home and make sure her kids were in bed because they had school in the morning.

Cookie mugged the shit out of her. "Bitch, I know you don't think you finna eat my pussy with all this heat shooting through these vents? My shit is not fresh and I'm banking that yours ain't either. So, we gone have to miss out on this lil' gee he talking about 'cuz I definitely ain't finna have the first time I eat some pussy tasting like fish." She closed her eyes and made a   disgusted face.

Trixie was irritated. "Dang, fa real? You finna make us miss out on this money like that?" Caspur was so high now that he was dozing off. His head kept on snapping backwards, then he would jolt awake. "Bitch, I ain't making you miss shit. I ain't finna eat yo' funky pussy. A gee is not worth all of that. That won't even cover my car note payment, never mind the rent. So why would I do that?"

Trixie frowned. "Ugh, I hate you bougie ass bitchez. Hoez act like they better than   everybody. Make me sick. I can't believe I'm finna miss out on a whole ass gee. I got three kids. That is a lot of money to me. All my baby daddies are bums."

Cookie felt some type of way about that revelation. She sorta took a shine to Trixie's youngest daughter. The little girl was beautiful, just like her mother. She had caramel skin and natural green eyes. She was three years old. Her father had come to the club one time and kicked the shit out of Trixie because she had been hounding him about the child support for that month. She remembered it was horrible. He had put on a show for all to see. When it was all said and done, he'd snatched up their daughter and left for two whole days without contacting Trixie.

She had been too afraid to call the police on him, too. Cookie felt herself ready to relent. She didn't want to be the reason Trixie wasn't able to provide for her children in any way and the thousand dollars would help her.

"Man, fuck the bitch. We'll just rape her

Cashville style, baby. You know how we get down," Caspur mumbled. "I'll give you three gees and this bitch don't get shit" He ran his hand over his face and opened his eyes. "Ya heard me? "

"Three gees?" Trixie asked, looking over her shoulder at him. She was beyond excited. She didn't know if she could take Cookie or not, but she was damn well finna try for three thousand dollars. "Three bands, bitch. Ya boy ain't stutter. Let's fuck this bitch right now," he mumbled and started to get up to close the partition.

Trixie took Cookie's knees and forced them apart, while Caspur knelt beside her on the seat and held her down. "Reach under there and pull her panties off, Caspur. Come on, I'm gone help you as much as I can," she said, biting into Cookie's thigh to force her to open her legs. "Why is y'all doing this to me?" Cookie whimpered. "Stop! Please!"

Chapter 14

Greed dug deeply with the shovel one more time before scooping the dirt and tossing it over his shoulder. In back of him he could hear Jersey crying and it was breaking his heart. The worst sound in the world was that of his wife sobbing. He could barely take it. After he scooped the last bit of dirt, he climbed out of the grave just as the rain started to come down hard on them.

It was 4 am in the morning. It was freezing cold out and they were in the Pine Grove woods about to bury Ajani who had died five days ago. An old friend of Greed's did them the service of embalming his body and provided them with an all-white and gold casket. Greed, Aiden and Rayjon had dug the grave themselves. Now it was time to bury him and Jersey was taking it hard.

Jersey reached in and kissed Ajani on the forehead again and rubbed his chest that had been ripped to shreds. She couldn't believe that her son was gone, her little baby boy that she'd given birth to it seemed just like yesterday, her little Leo. She broke down to her knees and shook her head.

Rayjon came over and rubbed her back, helping her to stand up. The wind picked up its speed, causing their faces to become frozen. It was November and winter was in full effect.

"Momma, its gone be okay. He's in a better place. He's with dad's mother now. You already know she gone hold him down."

Jersey shook her head. "But he's my baby, not hers. He's my little man and I want him back. Please get him back, Rayjon. He's our Apple Head." She cried, nearly falling to her knees if it wasn't for Rayjon holding her up.

Averie walked over to Ajani's casket and looked down at him. She couldn't believe that he was dead. First, her son and now, his father. She wondered if his whole lineage was just cursed or something. Emotionally, she felt nothing. She wasn't sad that he was gone. She wasn't happy either. She simply felt like he was a chapter in her life that needed to be closed.

It took them twenty minutes to say their good-byes to him and another forty before they   lowered him into the ground and covered him with dirt. Now that Ajani was buried, Greed was ready to find King and murder him, but after he took care of Money first. Word was out that he was back in the States and Greed was going to take a trip to Connecticut.

* * *

Rayjon kissed Jersey on the forehead before clos-ing the door and walking into the arms of Averie. She laid her head on his chest and rubbed his stomach. "Are you okay, baby?"

Rayjon held her as they walked and ended up in the kitchen. He was starving and had to feed his stomach. He'd hadn't eaten in damn near two days. He was missing his brother and was caught up in a dilemma, deciding if he should just up and leave or to tell his parents first. He didn't want to seem dis-loyal to the family, but at the same time he wanted more. He didn't want to have to always kill and hunt.

He wanted to live life. He wanted a family and he wanted to   enjoy love with Averie.

"I'm good, baby. I'm just starving right now. You feel like cooking something?" He opened the refrigerator and looked around.

Averie shrugged her shoulders. "I'm fine with that. What do you have a taste for?"

Rayjon came and sat back at the table. "It don't even matter. Whatever you feel like   whipping up." He felt his stomach growl like it had an attitude or something.

Averie decided she'd make him a nice cheesy omelet and hash browns. She figured some nice sausages and a cup of orange juice outta do the trick. "So baby, have you talked to them yet or decided what you're going to do?" she asked nervously. She knew that the hard part for him was telling his parents that he was leaving. After he got over that hump, it would be smooth   sailing for them.

Rayjon lowered his head. "N'all, but I been trying to find an opening to do that. I think I'm gone holler at my mom's first because she's more understanding. My pops won't be trying to hear what I'm talking about because he bent on revenge, so you already know how that go."

Averie cracked three eggs into the metal bowl and started whipping them. She added some shredded American cheese and a little mozzarella. "Yeah, I think mom understands everything with an open heart. She's a good woman. I hate to see her so down and broken, but I know she'll bounce back. It never takes her long."

Rayjon stood up and stretched. "To be honest,

I'm scared to even tell them."

Jersey stepped into the kitchen and tightened her robe around her body. "Tell us what?" Her mouth was dry, so she'd gotten up to get her something to drink. She had been listening to their conversation for the last three minutes trying to make out what they were talking about.

Rayjon nearly jumped out of his skin. He looked from his mother, then over to Averie. "Ma, we were just talking about some stuff. I ain't ready to bring it to you just yet, but I will in a minute once I get my head on straight," he said, feeling sick.

Jersey reached into the refrigerator and pulled out the apple juice. "You finna tell me what you talking about right now or else Averie about to witness me whooping your tail for the first time. Then I'm gone whoop hers," she said matter of factly.

Averie frowned and imagined what that would be like. She remembered when Jersey had whooped her cousin Stacey after she found out she was pregnant with Ajani's baby. She knew the woman would have no problem whooping her ass. She just didn't think she could sit back and accept it, but if she had to she would have.

"Matter of fact, Averie why don't you be woman enough to tell me what's going on," Jersey challenged. Averie immediately looked to Rayjon and he lowered his head. "Don't look at him. Look at me. Let's do this shit like women. Tell me what's going on. What, you scared or something? You ain't woman enough to stand on your own two feet in honor of my son?"

Averie flipped the omelet in the skillet, letting it

cook for a few moments before sliding it on to a plate in front of Rayjon. In the other skillet, she smashed down the sausage patties, watching the grease pop from under them before taking them out of the pan and placing them on Rayjon's plate. She then went into the refrigerator and grabbed the grape jelly. "Look momma, I love Rayjon and I don't want nothing happening to him or for him to get caught up in anything else that's going on around here. He's my heart and I will die for him any day. But we're trying to figure out how to tell you we're leaving and going to Miami indefinitely so we can have a better life than this."

"Wait, don't say it like that. Momma, what she mean is—"

Jersey held up her hand. "Hush, I know exactly what she mean. I'm not stupid." Jersey mugged her with anger before turning her head to the side. "So, you think that you can just come into this family and take my baby away from me? You think that you can take ownership of both of my sons, then when one goes down, you can just have the other one and leave me with   nothing? Huh?"

Averie finished pouring Rayjon's orange juice with her eyes now bugged out of her head. "Wait, momma. It's not like that. I just—"

"You just what? You think you can replace me? You think you can do a better job for him than I can? You think you're the new woman around here that's gone make sure that I don't have no sons left?" She frowned and slammed her hand on the table. "Well speak up!"

Averie was staring to panic. The last thing she

wanted was to have any problems with Jersey. She knew that the woman was crazy, just like the men in their family. She tried to put her thoughts together in order to properly defend herself. "Umm. Umm. Mom, well all I'm saying is—"

Jersey shook her head. "You mean to tell me that this is who you banking on? You think this girl is worthy of you running away with? She can't even stand up for herself." She sucked her teeth. "Lil girl, you gone have to have a lot more heart than that if you think you finna take my place. I have never folded when it came to Greed. If anybody asked me what my place was in regards to him, I stood on my gangsta and was ready to die for my man, still am. You standing there looking all soft and shit, acting like you care about my son. How can you when you can't even stand on your own two feet as a woman?" Jersey spoke through clenched teeth.

Quiet as kept, she really loved Averie and she was happy that they were together. She felt that out of all the women out there that Averie would be the one to hold her son down one hundred percent. She didn't doubt her for a second. Her only gripe with the girl was that she didn't stand up for herself enough. Even after she killed Game, she still didn't act like she was a part of the family.

Averie was so tired of everybody picking on her. They just would not leave her alone. All she wanted was to have Rayjon all to herself. She didn't want to share him, and she wanted to make sure that they escaped out of New Jersey with their lives intact. If that meant that she had to go through Jersey in order for all of that to take place, then she was all for it.

"You know what, Momma Jersey? I love Rayjon and he's my heart. There is nothing in this world that I wouldn't do for him and I know for a fact that we're going to be together for a very long time. He's my world and I want him out of the game, point blank period. We're going to Miami. In fact, we're leaving first thing in the morning. He's my job now and I will die   protecting him, just like I know he'd die doing the same for me. So n'all, I ain't trying to replace you. I'm just trying to make sure that you have at least one breathing child left, so when you're done with this underworld crap, he'll be able to wrap you in his arms because the both of you deserve that."

Jersey looked at her for a long time without saying a word. She felt that Averie had finally stood up for herself. It made her proud. She secretly wanted Rayjon to get the hell out of New Jersey and away from all of the drama. She had been trying to find a clever way to get him away from it all, so she thanked Jehovah for Averie.

Rayjon lowered his head before looking up and eyeing his mother closely. He knew she was a goon, so he was waiting for her to snap out. He loved Averie to death. No matter what, he was getting on that plane whenever she did. He saw himself being with her for the rest of his life.

Jersey reached and pulled Averie to her, wrapping her arms around her neck. "I love you so much, girl. You better watch over my baby because he'll meet that Reaper to protect you. Y'all belong together. By the time I meet y'all down there, there had better be a bun in this oven. You hear me?"

Averie blinked tears, holding on to her neck even

tighter.

* * *

Heinous waited until Cherry took her keys out of her pocket to open her car door before he jumped out of his truck that was parked next to hers. He wrapped his arm around her neck and threw her into the passenger's seat of his truck, putting a .44 Desert eagle to her head and   climbing over. "Ya shut up gal or mi blow ya brains right out."

He got behind the wheel, started the truck, and pulled off while she whimpered in the   passenger's seat. Cherry was scared out of her mind. She didn't know what he wanted with her. She was just prayed that he wasn't going to kill her just to make a statement. "Heinous, I don't want no problems with you. Why are you doing this to me? "

He looked over at her and snarled. "You American girls so weak. Back in my country, the gals know betta than to whimper in the face of adversity. You take it like eh woman, even if you're gonna die. It's the Jamaican way."

All Cherry heard was him say was "even if you are going to die". So she took that to mean that he was getting ready to kill her, turning hysterical. "Oh God, please don't kill me, Mr.   Heinous. I ain't got shit to do with you and Chris or King or whoever you don't like. I'm just a stripper for them. I follow orders."

He curled his upper lip. "You're disgusting, a peasant." He spit a big green loogey in her face. "Shut up and tell me where King's family stays."

Cherry felt the hot ball of spit smack into her cheek. She wanted to throw up. Not only was she disgusted, but she was pissed off. Spitting on somebody was the nastiest thing you could possibly do. She wiped her face with the sleeve of her Moschino wind breaker, looking at   Heinous with absolute hatred. "If I give you the address to where he live, are you gone let me go?"

He made a left and pressed down on the gas, increasing his speed. "Type it into my GPS. I'll decide your fate later on."

* * *

China finished stapling King's head, leaned over and kissed each wound. "There you go,   baby. How does it feel?"

King sat up and stretched his arms over his head yawning. He had a splitting headache. Even after all of the work China had put into him the last two days, he still felt like he was in pain. "I'm good. I think I just need to rest my eyes a little bit, then I'ma finish this mission and get my ass back to the Windy City, my homeland." He stepped in front of the mirror and touched the staples. "When are the Young Radicals supposed to arrive out here?"

The Young Radicals were a crew of cold-hearted assassins that King and Chris had trained to be worse than them. They were comprised of starving project kids that grew up in the
same project buildings as he and Chris. So there was a strong sense of loyalty there.

"They supposed to arrive in a few hours. I already

gave them the order that you wanted them on bitness. Mickey is making the trip personally with his special crew. So you already know what that mean."

Mickey was King's uncle, the man that had taught him everything he needed to know about the game. Mickey was a calculating lunatic.

King smiled. "Then everything about to go the way it's supposed to. I wanna take a good look at Greed personally."

Chapter 15

Cherry covered her mouth to keep from screaming. She could not believe what was going on. She watched Heinous grab Nicole by the throat, stab her in the stomach with a knife, and split her wide open before punching his fist into the incision, yanking her baby out of her. It was almost too much to believe.

As soon as he ripped her baby out, he threw it to the floor. Nicole fell to her face, shaking like a fish out of water as blood pooled around her. She was only four months pregnant, so the baby lay beside her barely moving before he jumped into the air, bringing his feet down on the little girl's chest, bussing it wide open. Nicole was King's baby mother and a female he grew up with alongside of him, Chris and China. His mother introduced them to each other. Now she was dead and so was their child.

Chris's 6 year-old twins were under the table with their hands over their ears. They were afraid for their lives. The little boy and girl stopped and hugged each other before Heinous grabbed the little boy by the leg, pulling him from under the table while he screamed.

Heinous picked him up by the throat and threw him against the wall, bussing his head wide open. The little boy shook on the floor with plasma running down his cheek. He looked like he was in so much pain. Heinous walked over to him and picked him back up. "Yo' daddy has a hard time listening to me and because of that, you are forced to pay the consequences."

He threw him into the wall again, leaving a big hole in it before he fell to the floor crying his little eyes out. Heinous didn't give a fuck. He had watched numerous kids being killed back in Kingston, Jamaican. Children that the world seemed to not care about, so he didn't feel like he should have to care about the children of America.

Christian tried to crawl away from the big man, but his body would not move. It hurt so bad and he didn't wanna play anymore. He was scared and he wanted his daddy. The man to him was scary. He felt himself being lifted into the air, turned upside down and brought to the ground so fast before he felt the impact that knocked his life out of him. Heinous power bombed the little boy into the floor again and again.

Boom! Boom! Boom! Boom!

Slamming his back on to the marble floors, he shattered his spine and cracked his head wide open. He turned and looked under the table at the little girl. "You're next little bitch! "

She shook her head. "No! No! Please!" She got up to run away, but he grabbed her by her ponytail, yanking her backward. Her feet went up into the air before she fell on her back. He slid the knife across the floor to Cherry and upped the .44 Desert Eagle out of the small of his back, aiming it at her one hundred times.

"I want you to call Chris right now, then hand me the phone. Then I want you to stab her a hundred times, here and here," he said, pointing to her throat and chest.

Cherry threw up in her mouth, some dripping off

of her chin. She was devastated. She felt like the world was coming to an end. There was no way possible she could kill Chris's daughter, Christen. She was her godmother and on top of that, her father's mistress.

"Please don't make me do this, Heinous. I will do anything else, but not this," she whimpered, holding the bloody knife in her hand.

He cocked back the Desert Eagle. "Bitch, you ain't got a choice. Do it now! Call him!" he roared with hatred.

Cherry called him, Facetiming before she threw Heinous the phone. Chris accepted it. Once Heinous' face popped up on the screen, he wanted to snap. His first thoughts were that Cherry had quit working for him, switching over to the Jamaican. "What the fuck you want, nigga?"

Heinous curled his lip. "This is what happens when you don't listen to Jamaica." He turned to Cherry. "Do it!" he yelled, holding the phone so Chris could get a clear view.

Chris saw his daughter come into the picture, then Cherry with a big knife over her head. "I'm sorry, Chris!" She brought it down with all of her might. He saw his daughter's blood pop
into the air. Then Cherry brought the knife down again, forcing more blood to shoot up.

"Oh shit! Not my baby! Not my baby girl!"

He wanted to faint. He couldn't take his eyes away from the screen. Cherry went berserk, stabbing her over and over again, counting out loud all the way to one hundred. Then she sat back with the knife in her hands, blood all over her face, crying.

Heinous looked into the phone. "Jamaica. Jamai-caaaaaaaa, yeah. Jamaica, Jamaica!" He threw the phone to the floor with all of his might. He grabbed Cheery by the hair and took her upstairs where they had left King's son Prince tied up. "He's coming with me and you let King and Chris know that this is what war looks like." He grabbed her by the throat before tossing her toward the hallway. "Now go!"

* * *

August jumped over the fence, ran behind the bodyguard, and slit his throat before throwing him to the grass. He took the 9-millimeter off of the man's hip and placed it on his own hip. To his left, he could see his brother Aiden snapping a bodyguard's neck, then low crawling to the next one.

Greed kept his back to the house, slowly moving along the side of it. He looked into the first window and saw there was a maid inside vacuuming the rugs. He couldn't really see anyone besides her but figured all of Money's family had to be home. He dropped down and made his way to the back of the yard with the hopes that one of the patio doors would be open.

Aiden crawled on his knees. As soon as he got within arm's reach of the guard, he took the knife and slammed it up into his prostate before ripping it backward toward his ass crack.

The man hollered and fell to his knees. Aiden got behind him and snapped his neck, leaving his chin behind his back. August got closer to the door. There he saw a guard talking on a cellphone, flirting with what had to be a woman. The man was smiling and everything. He almost looked goofy to him. August shrugged his shoulders, figuring that the kill was going to be too easy. He came out of the bushes and walked right towards the man like it wasn't anything out of the ordinary.

"Hey, what are you doing?" he hollered, turning off the cellphone and sliding it in his pocket.

August spun on his feet and stopped in front of him before jamming the knife into his throat, twisting the handle three times.

The guard could feel the blade hollowing out his throat. It felt like he had swallowed a bunch of sharp objects. He tried to swallow but it hurt so bad that he started jumping up and down in agony.

Aiden came from behind him and stabbed him ten times in the throat, yanking their knife out of him and giving it back to his little brother August.

The sun was shining bright. Even though it felt like it was only about thirty degrees outside, Money managed to have his pool uncovered. It looked like blue mouthwash. August smiled at it and had thought of taking a swim before he left the place.

* * *

Greed tried the handle to the patio door and just like he figured, it opened right up. He stepped inside, sliding the pistol from the small of his back. He could still hear the vacuum
Going which told him that the maid was in the front of the house.

He made his way into the kitchen and saw his son Curtis entering and opening the   refrigerator.

When he saw him he froze.

"Wait a minute. Who are you?" he asked, looking suspicious.

Greed raised the gun and aimed it at him. "Come here or I'm popping you."

Curtis said to himself *fuck that*, deciding to take his chance. He turned to run out of the kitchen but ran right into the arms of Aiden. Aiden wrapped the teenaged boy into a bear hug, then head butted him so hard, he shattered the bones in his face. He cocked back and did it again and again, harder and harder until Curtis died in his arms. Then he dropped him to the floor and stepped over him, nodding with his head upstairs.

August grabbed a piece of bread off of the counter and ate it. He looked around the big mansion duly impressed. He stepped over Curtis's body and watched his uncle and brother go up the stairs. Greed pointed at the maid and he nodded. He slowly crept up behind her and shook his head. He really didn't like killing older women and he didn't know why, but he knew he had to get it over and done with.

Esther pushed the vacuum cleaner back and forth and enjoyed the music coming through her new Beats by Dre headphones. Her old Patti Labelle was sounding good. She was so thankful for them. All she had to do was fold the laundry and her day was done. She couldn't wait to get home and relax. It was her husband's night to cook and he was thinking barbeque. She couldn't wait.

Just as she turned the vacuum cleaner off, she felt something stinging her neck, but thought nothing of it. She felt it again and immediately placed her fingers to where she felt the pain. When she pulled them back, she damn near had a heart attack. They were wet with blood. She was confused. "How the hell can that be?" she said out loud.

August took a step back after slicing the woman's throat two quick times back and forth. He loved watching people die, not necessarily older women, but since he had committed the murder, it intrigued him to see what she was going to do.

Esther felt her neck peeing. Then she got dizzy and started to stumble around, looking for the wall to hold her up, but it was nowhere in sight. She felt her windpipes filling up with blood. It felt like she was drowning. The room started to spin, her heart beating faster than it ever had before. Her lungs were working overtime yet were clogged. She fell to her knees reaching towards the sky, begging for help in her mind, but no sound came out. Finally, she fell to her face after her lungs exploded and her heart stopped working. A pool of blood formed around her left cheek.

August turned his head to the side, smiled, and got up. Every time he saw a person die, it got better and better. Killing was the best to him.

* * *

Money dug deeper into his baby's momma's pussy, trying to put his name on her spine. It was so wet he couldn't get enough of it. He cocked his back and pounded forward again and again. He had her cuffed into a little ball, blowing her back out.

"Umm shit, baby. You killing this pussy today.

You killing this shit just like I like it," Juanita moaned with her mouth wide open.

Money closed his eyes and pumped harder and harder. He was going to do his best to pullout before he came. As good as the pussy was, he still wasn't trying to have another kid by her. He felt like she was ratchet at the end of the day. He loved his son Curtis, but his mother he could do without.

Aiden to the meat hook and slammed it into Money's back deeply before yanking him off of her.

"Ahhhh! What the fuck is that in my back!" he hollered with tears rolling down his cheeks.

Juanita screamed at the top of her lungs before Greed picked her up by the throat and slammed her into the closet door. "Bitch, shut the fuck up or its gone get real ugly for you. Do you understand that?" He dropped her to the floor and put his Tims on her neck.

Juanita tried her best to not move. His big boot was choking her and she was having a hard time breathing, but she was happy to be alive. The pain was so unbearable in Money's back that he was crying like a newborn baby. He had never felt anything like it until Aiden picked him up in the air with both hands on the handle. "Ahhh! Please make it stop! I can't take this shit! I'm sorry niggas. Damn!" he hollered, shitting on himself.

Aiden wiggled the hook out of his back and looked at the holes he had made. It was two huge holes that were pooling blood. He liked the sight of it. It meant that Money was feeling pain. To him that's what it was all about, pain and more pain.

Greed came over and squatted down in front of

Money just as August came back into the room. "Bitch nigga, I ain't kill you the first time, but this time I won't make that mistake. You just couldn't let sleeping dogs lie huh?"

Money looked up to him in serious pain. He squinted his eyes, and then Greed's face came into view. He shitted some more, knowing that it was all over for him. Word was out that when it came to hitting niggas, Greed was a beast. He'd slipped before and caught 9 slugs. Now he was caught in his own home with no security around. He knew it was all over. "Greed, yo kid. I ain't even on that shit, man. I can't fuck wit' you man. I left that shit alone back in the past. It's 2018, son."

Greed grabbed him by the throat and picked him up, standing him on his own two feet. He cocked back and hit him.

Bam!

After punching him straight in the mouth, he knocked three of his teeth down his throat. Money started to choke right away before Aiden picked him up and slammed his stomach down on his knee so hard, he spit the teeth across the room, falling on his back in pain. Aiden grabbed him back up and threw him down all over again in front of Greed's Tims.

"Yo' this shit ain't right, kid. I ain't fucking wit' you, Greed. Why you doing this shit .to me?"

Greed knelt down and grabbed him by his throat again. "Bitch nigga, who the fuck is King and why you got him hunting my family?" He pulled the scalpel out of the sheath in his waist and held it in front of Money's face so he could see the blade gleam. "Make sure you answer correctly or it's about to get real fucked up around here."

Money winced in pain. He didn't know who the fuck King was or what Greed was talking about. He wanted to come up with a story to tell him just to get him off of his ass, but nothing came to mind.

"Word is bond. I don't know no nigga named King. I know what I don't know is what Sun got going on wit' yo' family, Boss. But it ain't got shit to do wit' me. I left our beef back in Sing-Sing. That's my word."

Greed curled his lip. He knew he was lying. He grabbed him by the head and sliced him across the face five times.

Whick! Whick! Whick! Whick! Whick!

Money felt the stinging slices and started to scream like an Opera singer. It felt like he was being hit with little bolts of lightning. He tried to jerk his head back, but it was no use. Greed had him held firmly. He stood up and looked down on the man, stomping him in the face.

"Bitch ass nigga, I lost my son to that nigga. You gone pay one way or the other." He put the scalpel into the palm of his hand and balled his fist with the blade sticking between his fingers. "Hold his head, nephew."

Aiden picked up his head and held it firmly between his hands, eyeing his uncle closely. He was what he wanted to be. Greed was his idol. A pure killer. No nonsense and all about their family. He wanted a title like his. A name that would ring all over the world.

August knelt down so he could watch the murder up close and personal. He felt giddy in the inside. He couldn't wait to watch the man slowly die. He couldn't wait until his brother took over the Ski Mask Cartel and they stepped out on their own, creating their own legacy.

Greed envisioned his son in his mind, remembering what it looked like to watch him be murdered. His heart grew heavy, and then he looked at Money with pure hatred. "Fuck you then, bitch nigga. Rest in hell, I'll see you when I get there."

He slammed his fist into his eye, popping it immediately. Then he punched him again in the face, over and over again while he screamed and hollered because the pain was the truth.

Money felt the blade enter into his eye and saw blue lightning before it exploded. Then the stabbing pains started over and over again. He felt the blade rip through his muscles and tissues, puncturing the meat and slicing through his veins. It was so horrible he didn't know what to do.

August sat still as the blood popped all over his face. He didn't want to miss a single stab. He kept on watching Money's eyes to see if the life had left them yet. For him, that was the best part, when the life left out of a man or a woman. It was like the changing of seasons. It was beautiful to him and he would wait all night until Money's seasons had finally changed.

Before it was all said and done, Greed punched him over 300 times in the face. Stabbing away the meat of his grill until he was left with nothing but bloody bones.

Chapter 16

Mickey cocked his foot back and kicked in the door with all of his might.

Booom!

It splintered. He cocked back and kicked again.

Booom!

The door flew inward and he waved his hand forward, ordering the Young Radicals to file into the house he was told Greed's wife was staying by her lonesome. He'd been given word that she was in the process of grieving which made her vulnerable. It would be an easy kill. At the same time they were sweating her, his other crew should have been sweating Averie's house. Both moves were supposed to take place at the same time, and then it was back to Chicago for them, in and out.

He knelt down and tapped the trigger to activate the green beam that was on the top of his fully automatic DSK. A weapon he referred to as the Dutch Bitch. It had 60 in the clip and it spit rapidly.

* * *

Rayjon had been up all night. He couldn't sleep, thinking about his brother as he tried to wrap his head around the fact that he and Averie would be leaving this life behind. He didn't even know what that looked like. For as long as he had been alive, his life had always been about family. One unit. Loyalty of the bloodline. Now, he was set to leave it all behind and his family in crisis. It made him sick to his stomach and he was having a hard time letting go.

He took another long swallow from the Hennessy and wiped his mouth, looking out of the attic window at the moon. He wondered if there really was a heaven. If so, he hoped that his brother was there at that moment, looking down on him probably getting ready to rob some Angels or something. He smiled at that as a tear sailed down his cheek.

"I miss you, kid and I'll never forget you. You was my heart, dawg and still is."

He took another swallow and stood up, looking down on to the street as the black van pulled in front of the house. About four men filed out in all white. They were heavily armed. He dropped the bottle of alcohol, with his eyes bugged out of his head.

"Holy shit! Averie!" he said out loud before breaking his neck to get downstairs.

* * *

J-Rock was the second in command of his unit for the Young Radicals. This was the branch that King snatched away from the B.D.s and renamed them the Young Radicals, the Murder Mob division. He was a high yellow, bald headed lunatic with nothing but murder on his mind   alongside of money. He took one step back and with all of his might, he kicked the door right by the lock.

Whooom!

It flew open and he ordered his troops to move in front of him while he stayed back and waited to hear shots. His job was to wait until they did their thing, leaving him to finish off   anybody that made it through them. This was going to be a bloody night and he was ready.

* * *

Rayjon rushed into the bedroom and smacked Averie on the ass before running to the closet and grabbing his 90 shot Mach. 90. He threw two clips in his pocket and flipped the switch on the beam that was located on the top of the machine gun. His heart was beating fast. Sweat poured down his forehead and he felt like he could barely. The only person he thought about was his brother. He tried to get a hold of himself. Breathing was becoming difficult.

"Averie! Get up, baby! Get up right now and get dressed!"

He threw on his bulletproof vest, and ran over to the bed and pulled the covers back. Averie sat up with sleep in her eyes. She was groggy since they hadn't had a decent night's sleep in nearly a month because there was so much stuff going on in the family. "Baby, why are you waking me up? I just got to sleep," she whined.

Rayjon ripped her nightgown down the middle, exposing her breasts, then took the extra vest and slid it over her head.

"You gotta hurry up! Them niggas is here and they coming to kill us. They just pulled up, ma! Let's go!"

Whooom!

They heard the door being kicked in. It almost sounded like a gunshot blast. Then it sounded like a bunch of boots were stomping through the house.

Averie slid the vest all the way on and dropped to the floor beside Rayjon with tears in her eyes. "Oh my God! Oh my God! Baby, what do we do?"

He pulled her down beside him more firmly, handed her a 9-millimeter. "You aim for a mafucka's head. The gun gone give you a lil' kick, but you remember that your life is on the line, so you handle it. Get in that closet right there. I gotta protect home."

Whoom!

It sounded like they were ripping the downstairs apart. Rayjon knew it couldn't be long before they made their way up the stairs. If he remembered correctly, he had only seen four men get out of the van, but he figured that there had to be at least five because they had to have a driver waiting to pull away when they jumped back in.

He had two clips that were 90 rounds apiece. That's 180 for five people. His gat spit three bullets at a time, which meant that every time he pulled the trigger he had to count down from 60, because 60 pulls would equal the full 180 rounds. Shit was getting real.

He ran into the hallway and fell to his stomach, low crawling until he got to the bathroom that was the first door when you got to the top of the stairs. From there, he would be able to see them coming up them and have a direct shot.

* * *

Whino frowned and after kicking open the pantry and not finding anybody hiding inside. He was ready to kill something. He didn't want to be out in New Jersey all week. He was one of those niggas that didn't like to leave his homeland. He'd been in Chicago all his life and never wanted to leave. A project kid that ran under King and Chris's Young Radicals. He was eating and down for the cause.

He left out of the pantry and stayed low. He came to the stairs and looked up. He tapped Pito on the shoulder and pointed up. Pito nodded then Whino slowly made his way up the stairs hoping the soon to be victims were still sleep although he couldn't see how with all the noise they'd made downstairs.

Two more steps and he was at the top. He looked behind him at Pito, putting his finger to where his lips would be in the white ski mask telling him to hush. He turned to look down the long hallway and it felt like he heard a loud popping sound like gunfire. He saw fire coming from a room in front of him, feeling like more punches to his face. He thought about upping his weapon, but he started falling backwards in slow motion with a splitting headache. His brain felt like it was splitting in two and then everything got dark.

Pito saw Whino's brains shoot out the back of his head, not once but twice. The man's head twisted all the way around on his shoulders before he jumped into the air with his white mask ripped apart. His body fell into his and Pito nearly lost his mind. That was his first cousin. They had grown up together and were real close.

He turned around to help him and heard the loud gunshots before feeling about 40 slugs attack his back and neck. He screamed and tried to turn around to shoot, but his head exploded as more than six bullets ripped into his cheek, knocking off his face. His last thoughts were of him wishing he'd never came to New Jersey in the first place.

Rayjon stood up and looked down on them. "Bitch ass niggas. It ain't sweet." He held the smoking machine gun, running back into the room where he'd made Averie hide in the closet. "Baby, come on. Let's get the fuck out of here," he said, pulling her up by the hand.

Averie's heart was beating so fast she could barely breathe. She already had asthma, praying she didn't break out into an episode. They needed to get the fuck out of that house. The attack was real.

Rayjon looked down the hallway and saw that it was still clear. "Come on, baby. Let's go into the room across the hall and jump down from the balcony in there. It's the only way.

Averie nodded. She trusted his judgment. She couldn't believe how levelheaded he was at a time like that. It made her love him even more. He grabbed her hand as they ran across the hall with him throwing her into the room first.

Boo-wa! Boo-wa! Boo-wa! Boo-wa! Boo-wa! Boo-wa!

A bullet slammed into his chest and knocked him off his feet, breaking two of his ribs   immediately. A shotgun had blasted.

"Noooo!" Averie screamed and fell to her knees before jumping up.

Wando ran down the hall at full speed, stopping right in front of Rayjon leveling the   Masburg after pumping it. "Bitch ass nigga, you kilt my lil' cousins.

Rest in hell!'"

Boom! Boom! Boom! Boom! Boom! Boom!

"Ahhhhh! Leave my man alone! Ahhhh!'"

Boom! Boom! Boom!

Fire spit from her gun, lighting the room up. The first bullet slammed into Wando's forehead, making him stand straight up. It went into his eyebrow and knocked a chunk of his forehead off. The next one went into his nose and punched his brain out of his head. By the time the third   bullet slammed into his cheek, he had forgotten his own name and he couldn't feel any pain. He dropped the shotgun and stood up as more and more of his face disappeared, replaced by hole after hole. He fell on top of Rayjon. Averie pulled him off him, kneeling in front of her man.

"Daddy, are you okay? Please tell me that you're not dead!" she cried in a panic.

Rayjon laughed. "N'all, not yet, but we gotta get the fuck out of here. Come on," he said, corning to an aching stand.

Averie helped him up all the way, placing his arm around her neck for support.

Boom! Boom! Boom! Boom! Boom!

The first bullet hit Averie's shoulders, making her fall to her knees. The second slammed into her side and the third her thigh. The pain was so bad she couldn't help but to scream.

* * *

Greed opened his eyes. He could feel that something was wrong. He felt like something was wrong with his son. He sensed it. It was the same feeling he'd gotten regarding Ajani before he called him. "Fuck!"

He tried to shoot up in the bed, but discovered he was bound to it. He looked down and saw he was chained to the bed. Large metal chains were roped around him multiple times. He couldn't believe it how he had slept through something like that when the slightest of sounds usually woke him up immediately. He felt his head spinning, wondering what was going on. The room was pitch dark.

"Jersey! Jersey! Baby, where are you? Where are you, Momma?" he hollered, praying that his wife was okay.

The light slipped on and there was Aiden standing over the bed with his shirt off. He looked like a menacing high yellow body builder with a hundred tats. His chest heaved up and down, causing his abs to display themselves repeatedly. He looked like a straight goon. Greed mugged him. "Nephew, where is my wife?"

He nodded over his shoulder and August brought her into the room with duct tape around her mouth. He held a sharp deer-hunting knife to her throat, mugging Greed with hatred. "What's good, Unk?"

Greed looked from August then back to Aiden. "All y'all lives I've instilled nothing but loyalty and this is what it comes down to?"

"It's time I become head of my own cartel. You taught me that the only way I ever could was if you died or you passed the torch. Seeing as I'm only your nephew and Rayjon is still alive, the torch would go to him, but I'm ready now. I'm tired of being the tail.

I'm ready to be the head." He spit on the floor and mugged Greed. "With you as head, I done lost my mother, my grandmother and my cousin, not to mention a whole slew of other blood relatives. Now you don't even know who it is that's hunting us. You old, my nigga and it's time this family get a change of leadership."

Greed's heart broke in half. Aiden was the love of his life outside of his wife and sons. He loved his nephew nearly equal to his own sons. Ever since he was three years old, he had been a constant in his life, always making sure that he was well taken care, teaching him everything that he taught his own sons and taking extra time out to make sure that he understood everything. Aiden was the one person in his life that he just knew would never cross him.

"Now Unk, you know like I know that ain't no bitch in me and if I was to attack you while you're tied to the bed like that, I would never be honored as a great like you. So, what I wanna do is for us to fight to the death. The last man standing is the head."

Greed looked at him for a long time before nodding his head. That sounded more like the kid he had raised. Keeping shit gangsta and fighting for what he wanted. He couldn't wrap his head around the first thoughts he had of him going out like a coward.

"What's this shit you shot me up with to make me sleep so hard?" he asked, feeling a little funny.

Aiden frowned. "It's called Proxin. It ain't gone affect your fighting at all. It's just a mild sedative to help a person sleep more soundly." He walked towards his uncle with the key to the locks. "So, do we have a deal?"

"Yo August, on some real shit, kid. Take that ma-fucking knife away from my wife's throat, boss. This ain't that."

August shook his head. "I can't do that. This what she told me to do. She told me to keep this knife to her throat because if y'all get to fighting, she gone help you and she gone wind up   killing me and my brother. Since she's our aunty, she said she preferred it this way. Right, Aunty Jersey?" She gave and an-gry look and nodded her head. "So, we got a deal or not?" Aiden asked, ready for the battle.

* * *

Mickey and his crew tore up the whole house only to find nothing. He swung at the air in anger and got on his phone to call King. The worst mission that he felt he could have been placed on was a blank one.

* * *

Averie fell against Rayjon with her eyes closed. Her body felt like a ton of bricks. He fell backwards into the room with her. Sitting her up against the wall, he started to panic, praying that none of her vi-tal organs were hit. He needed her so badly. Would do anything for her.

J-Rock knew he had hit at least one of them, but he was thinking both. He slammed new clips into his .45s, letting them bitchez bark as they ran in their di-rection, knocking chunks out of the wall already hyped up off the cocaine that he'd been tooting by the gram.

Ba-boom! Ba-boom! Ba-boom! Ba-boom!

Rayjon fell on his back, waiting for the masked gunmen to present himself. "Ahhh! I'm hit! Fuck I'm hit!" he hollered, setting the nigga up.

J-Rock barely heard his wails over the gun blasts, but just caught it. He smiled under his mask and ran full speed in their direction, slamming a new clip into his .45. He had murder on his mind, wanting to body both of them. It would make the mission so sweet.

He got to the end of the hallway where the door was wide open, turned to finish both of them off right before felt the blast knock his balls from his body.

Rayjon aimed the Mach .90 right at his nuts and squeezed the trigger.

Boom-Boom-Boom! Boom-Boom-Boom!

"Ahhhhh!" J-Rock screamed as he felt his dick and balls being blown off his body. It felt like he was being hit in the groin with a big ass brick again and again. The pain was so bad that he dropped to his knees and put his face against Rayjon's barrel, daring him to pull the trigger. Blood ran down his ass and dripped along his thighs. "Kill me! Kill me, now! I can't take this shit!" he screamed, going insane.

Rayjon bit into his bottom lip. "No problem."

Boom! Boom! Boom!

Chapter 17

Greed picked Aiden up and slammed him with all his might onto his back, knocking the wind out of his nephew. His head bounced off the ground and he rolled on to his side before getting right back up. His jaw was already broken, yet he kept on corning. "You can't fuck wit' me nephew. Boy, I raised you. Don't you get that?"

Aiden lowered his head and attacked, stopping in front of Greed. He knelt and punched him so hard in the nuts, he popped one of his testicles before putting him onto his shoulder, lifting him in the air and slamming him down on his back with so much force that he was paralyzed for a full minute. He stood over him breathing hard.

When Aiden punched Greed in the nut sack, it felt like he had been hit in the balls with a sledge-hammer. He felt his right testicle burst, imagining a balloon popping before the pain shot all the way up to his eyes watering them. Then he felt himself being hoisted into the air. Before he could defend himself, he was slammed down with so much force it felt like he had been hit by a city bus while trying to cross the street. His entire body locked up and he could barely breathe.

Jersey screamed, still duct taped over the mouth. She tried to break away from August to get to her man. She wanted to protect him, to help, to do anything. She imagined Aiden taking his life and she nearly passed out before fighting to break away.

August's eyes were opened wide. He wanted to

see what was going to happen next. He had never seen two cold-blooded killers go at one another. It was almost too good to be true. He wrapped his arms more firmly around his Aunt, holding her in place as Greed slowly made it to his feet.

Greed stood up with shooting pain emanating from his nut sack, almost hobbling him. He could barely walk without feeling like he wanted to pass out, but he had to go on. He knew Aiden would take no pity on him. He had trained him to be relentless. He threw up his guard and curled his upper lip. "Let's go, nephew. I ain't dead yet."

Aiden's mind was blank. He didn't see his uncle standing in front of him. All he saw was a roadblock to becoming the head of his own organization in his path. His uncle always told him that he would never be able to step out on to his own if he was alive because everything revolved around family, a family that Greed ran, and Aiden wanted that spot.

He stepped forward and swung a haymaker at Greed that was blocked, but then he jumped in the air and kicked Greed straight in the chest before falling to the ground and sweeping him off his feet. Greed hit the deck hard. Aiden jumped on top of him, punching him in the face again and again. It felt like he was being hit with concrete slabs. The back of his head bounced off the ground before he took all the fight in him to move. Aiden missed and hit the concrete hard, yanking his fist back and shaking it out.

Greed pumped his hips upward, sending Aiden forward. He head-butted him straight in the face, bussing his nose and mouth. He then flipped on top of him and started to rain down heavy blows that were knocking him senseless. Once he knocked him out, he stood up and grabbed the back of his head, slamming it into the ground under them, bussing his head wide open. He was about to stomp his face in with his Tims when Jersey screamed.

He turned around to see August holding a .45 to her forehead with tears in his eyes. "Don't make me do it, Unk. Please, don't make me kill her. I love my aunty. She is the best aunty in
the world. Please."

Jersey stood with her head tilted back, tears rolling down her cheeks. The duct tape stuck to one side of her jaw, barely hanging on. "You gone kill me, August? Huh? After all we've done for you and your brother over the years?"

August tightened his grip on the pistol. "I don't wanna do this Aunty, but I can't let him kill my brother. I need him. I don't know how Rayjon carrying on without Ajani, but I need Aiden. My mother dead and fuck my father. He's all I got, and I can't lose him."

Greed took a step forward and August put his finger over the trigger, looking like he was ready to pull it, making Greed stop in his tracks. "Yo chill, a'ight. Let's talk about this shit. Point that mafucka at me and take it off my baby. I know you can do that."

"Greed, watch out!" Jersey screamed.

Greed felt something slice across his neck once, then twice. Then he was lifted into the air and slammed on to his back, knocking the wind out of him. He couldn't breathe, and his eyes were bugged out of his head. Aiden stood up and looked down on him. He was flopping around like a fish with blood spurting up from his throat like a water sprinkler, kicking his legs, dying slowly.

Greed felt like his entire body was shutting down. He felt the blood pouring into his lungs choking him. His chest closed, and his eyes felt like they wanted to pop out of his head. He could hear his heart beating super loud in his ears, everything was going from black and white to different colors. It felt like a bunch of sticky hot water was puddling around his back.

Jersey broke away from August and fell to her knees, watching her husband jerk up and down like a fish. Blood poured out of his neck horribly. He looked like he was in so much pain. It broke her heart. She felt weak, like life was over.

All he had ever tried to do was make sure their family was straight, living above standard. He'd always treated her like a Queen. He spoiled her, giving her anything that she asked for. He fed her mentally and physically, making sure she knew she was always first in life. He'd never raised a hand to her above the waist. Just an overall great man. She felt she would never be able to go on without him.

He continued to flop around on the ground dying, choking on his own blood. Suffocating. Praying for death to take over him. Jersey kissed his lips.

"It's okay, baby. August give me the gun, now!" she screamed.

August was already breaking down. He loved his uncle with all his heart. At that time, he didn't care what Jersey did with the gun. If she killed him and Aiden, he felt that they deserved it. Things had gone too far. Greed had been the only father he had ever known. He slid the gun across the ground to her.

She caught it and wiped the tears out of her eyes. Leaning down, she kissed the hopping Greed again and rubbed his chest.

"It's okay, baby. I just want you to know that I love you and that my loyalty is real." She thought about Rayjon and Averie and it made her feel emptier. He didn't need her anymore. He had Averie and she was sure she would hold him down. Quiet as kept, she saw a lot herself in Averie. She knew her son was in good hands.

She took the pistol and put it into Greed's mouth, kissing him on the cheek before she pulled the trigger three times.

Boom! Boom! Boom!

The back of his head blew out and splattered the concrete. Then she took the gun and put it into her mouth and pulled the trigger.

Boom!

She saw the bright light. It felt like the top of her scalp jumped away from her head. She saw herself falling backwards before everything faded to black. Her last sights were of August and Aiden running to her towards her.

* * *

Rayjon wiped the tears away from his cheek after watching the whole event. He couldn't believe that his mother, father, and little brother were gone. He vowed revenge against Aiden and August. He promised that shit was far from over. He grabbed Averie's hand as they continued running down the alley after smashing his cellphone. He'd been able to track his parents using their cellphones. Now that they were gone, he had to figure something out. His cousins had to die, and he had to get his weight up.

* * *

King arrived back in Chicago nine hours after he'd gotten the news that his family had been murdered in cold blood by Heinous, the Jamaican. He walked into his home and saw the   aftermath, falling to his knees. Beside him, Chris grabbed both of his dead twins and fell to the ground holding them.

King blinked tears. This meant war. This meant that every muthafucka that he even thought was Jamaican had to die. It was time for a season of no mercy. His son had been snatched up, his other children murdered along with his right-hand man's. It was all unacceptable, refusing to honor it.

Chris slowly stood up with both of his murdered children in his arms. He frowned and   lowered his eyes. His nose crinkled and the look he gave King said that he was ready to go all out. No words had to be exchanged. They were having a full conversation just by looking at each other. King allowed the tears to drop from his chin before speaking. "It's time for Beast mode, my nigga. Beast muthafuckin' mode."

* * *

Heinous sat back and took a strong pull from the Jamaican ganja. He had an evil smile on his face as King's son sat on the table in front of him chopped up into little bitty pieces. He picked up the boy's head and turned it upside down. Taking his blunt, he dumped the ashes into the open part of the head where the neck used to connect to it. In the background, Bob Marley wailed through his speakers.

"Jamaica! Jamaicaaaaaaaa, yeah! Jamaica! Jamaicaaaaa!"

The End or The Beginning?

Submission Guideline.

Submit the first three chapters of your completed manuscript to ldpsubmissions@gmail.com, subject line: Your book's title. The manuscript must be in a .doc file and sent as an attachment. Document should be in Times New Roman, double spaced and in size 12 font. Also, provide your synopsis and full contact information. If sending multiple submissions, they must each be in a separate email.

Have a story but no way to send it electronically? You can still submit to LDP/Ca$h Presents. Send in the first three chapters, written or typed, of your completed manuscript to:

LDP: Submissions Dept
Po Box 870494
Mesquite, Tx 75187

DO NOT send original manuscript. Must be a duplicate.

Provide your synopsis and a cover letter containing your full contact information.

Thanks for considering LDP and Ca$h Presents.

Coming Soon from Lock Down Publications/Ca$h Presents

BOW DOWN TO MY GANGSTA

By **Ca$h**

TORN BETWEEN TWO

By **Coffee**

BLOOD STAINS OF A SHOTTA **III**

By **Jamaica**

WHEN THE STREETS CLAP BACK **III**

By **Jibril Williams**

STEADY MOBBIN

By **Marcellus Allen**

BLOOD OF A BOSS **V**

By **Askari**

LOYAL TO THE GAME **IV**

By **T.J. & Jelissa**

A DOPEBOY'S PRAYER **II**

By **Eddie "Wolf" Lee**

IF LOVING YOU IS WRONG… **III**

LOVE ME EVEN WHEN IT HURTS

By **Jelissa**

DAUGHTERS OF A SAVAGE

By **Chris Green**

SKI MASK CARTEL **II**

By **T.J. Edwards**

TRAPHOUSE KING

By **Hood Rich**

BLAST FOR ME **II**

RAISED AS A GOON **V**

By **Ghost**

A DISTINGUISHED THUG STOLE MY HEART **III**

By **Meesha**

ADDICTIED TO THE DRAMA **III**

By **Jamila Mathis**

LIPSTICK KILLAH **II**

By **Mimi**

WHAT BAD BITCHES DO

By **Aryanna**

THE COST OF LOYALTY **II**

By **Kweli**

A DRUG KING AND HIS DIAMOND **II**

By **Nicole Goosby**

Available Now

RESTRAINING ORDER **I & II**

By **CA$H & Coffee**

LOVE KNOWS NO BOUNDARIES **I II & III**

By **Coffee**

RAISED AS A GOON I, II,   III & IV

BRED BY THE SLUMS I, II, III

BLAST FOR ME

By **Ghost**

LAY IT DOWN **I & II**

LAST OF A DYING BREED

BLOOD STAINS OF A SHOTTA I & II

By **Jamaica**

LOYAL TO THE GAME

LOYAL TO THE GAME II

LOYAL TO THE GAME III

By **TJ & Jelissa**

BLOODY COMMAS I & II

SKI MASK CARTEL

By **T.J. Edwards**

IF LOVING HIM IS WRONG…I & II

By **Jelissa**

WHEN THE STREETS CLAP BACK I & II

By **Jibril Williams**

A DISTINGUISHED THUG STOLE MY HEART I & II

By **Meesha**

PUSH IT TO THE LIMIT

By **Bre' Hayes**

BLOOD OF A BOSS **I, II, III & IV**

By **Askari**

THE STREETS BLEED MURDER **I, II & III**

THE HEART OF A GANGSTA I II& III

By **Jerry Jackson**

CUM FOR ME

CUM FOR ME 2

CUM FOR ME 3

An **LDP Erotica Collaboration**

BRIDE OF A HUSTLA **I & II**

T.J. EDWARDS

THE FETTI GIRLS **I, II& III**
By **Destiny Skai**
WHEN A GOOD GIRL GOES BAD
By **Adrienne**
A GANGSTER'S REVENGE **I II III & IV**
THE BOSS MAN'S DAUGHTERS
THE BOSS MAN'S DAUGHTERS II
THE BOSSMAN'S DAUGHTERS III
THE BOSSMAN'S DAUGHTERS IV
A SAVAGE LOVE   **I & II**
BAE BELONGS TO ME
A HUSTLER'S DECEIT I, II
By **Aryanna**
A KINGPIN'S AMBITON
A KINGPIN'S AMBITION **II**
I MURDER FOR THE DOUGH
By **Ambitious**
TRUE SAVAGE
TRUE SAVAGE II
TRUE SAVAGE **III**
By **Chris Green**
A DOPEBOY'S PRAYER
By **Eddie "Wolf" Lee**
THE KING CARTEL **I, II & III**
By **Frank Gresham**
THESE NIGGAS AIN'T LOYAL **I, II & III**
By **Nikki Tee**

182

GANGSTA SHYT **I II &III**

By **CATO**

THE ULTIMATE BETRAYAL

By **Phoenix**

BOSS'N UP **I , II & III**

By **Royal Nicole**

I LOVE YOU TO DEATH

By Destiny J

I RIDE FOR MY HITTA

I STILL RIDE FOR MY HITTA

By **Misty Holt**

LOVE & CHASIN' PAPER

By **Qay Crockett**

TO DIE IN VAIN

By **ASAD**

BROOKLYN HUSTLAZ

By **Boogsy Morina**

BROOKLYN ON LOCK I & II

By **Sonovia**

GANGSTA CITY

By **Teddy Duke**

A DRUG KING AND HIS DIAMOND

A DOPEMAN'S RICHES

By Nicole Goosby

<u>BOOKS BY LDP'S CEO, CA$H</u>

<u>TRUST IN NO MAN</u>

<u>TRUST IN NO MAN 2</u>

<u>TRUST IN NO MAN 3</u>

<u>BONDED BY BLOOD</u>

<u>SHORTY GOT A THUG</u>

<u>THUGS CRY</u>

<u>THUGS CRY 2</u>

<u>THUGS CRY 3</u>

<u>TRUST NO BITCH</u>

<u>TRUST NO BITCH 2</u>

<u>TRUST NO BITCH 3</u>

<u>TIL MY CASKET DROPS</u>

<u>RESTRAINING ORDER</u>

<u>RESTRAINING ORDER 2</u>

<u>IN LOVE WITH A CONVICT</u>

<u>Coming Soon</u>

BONDED BY BLOOD 2

BOW DOWN TO MY GANGSTA

BLOODY COMMAS 3